Praise for Annmarie McKenna's Blackmailed

Gold Star Award! "Wow, all I can say is Ouch! This story is too hot to handle, which made me read it like a kid in a candy store, completely pumped up on the story. There is everything from bondage, domination and submission, as well as several blazing hot ménage a trois scenes. While this is not for the faint of heart, it is definitely a book for those who are looking for some loving yet wild sex. ...Overall, I could not put down this electrifying, deliciously intense novel with characters that tweaked my senses and sexual proclivities that left me burning with unreleased passion. I would highly recommend Blackmailed and feel it deserving of a Gold Star Award." ~ *Francesca Hayne, Just Erotic Romance Reviews*

"Blackmailed by Annmarie McKenna was an absolute delight to read! So delightful it made me sweat, and ache, and wish for two sexy heroes. Every girl needs a Cole Masters and Tyler Cannon! Two more loving, devoted and naughty heroes I have yet to meet; they put the H in hot!... Well written with extremely erotic love scenes, Blackmailed just kept me spell bound from beginning to end. Tastefully written love scenes and a bit of a surprise ending made for a wonderful read. I can't wait to see what else Ms. McKenna has in store for readers because I, for one, am now a fan of this author!" ~ *Talia Ricci, Joyfully Reviewed.com*

Blackmailed

Annmarie McKenna

A SAMHAIN PUBLISHING, LTD. publication.

Samhain Publishing, Ltd.
2932 Ross Clark Circle, #384
Dothan, AL 36301

Blackmailed
Copyright © 2006 by Annmarie McKenna
Cover by Scott Carpenter
Print ISBN: 1-59998-213-7
Digital ISBN: 1-59998-111-4
www.samhainpublishing.com

First Samhain Publishing, Ltd. electronic publication: May 2006
First Samhain Publishing, Ltd. print publication: August 2006

Dedication

Thank you –
Steve, my hubby who puts up with all my time on the computer,
Sasha, you know what "that's" about,
Sharis, Amanda, Colleen, Cathy, Anna, Ann,
And all my CORE buddies, who didn't get to read the sexy parts.
Mom—love you.
In memory of James Shaw.

Chapter One

Brianna Wyatt stared at the arrogant, red-faced man sitting across from her and snorted. She should have known better than to get into the limo with him. Her father, only in the sense he'd provided the sperm that had created her, was demented. She let her eyes fall to a speck on the red-carpeted floor.

He'd cast her aside for all her twenty-six years, and *now* he suddenly needed her?

"I will have a grandson, Brianna, my heir, and since you're the only legitimate vessel I have, you'll be the one to give him to me!"

Where did her father get these ideas anyway? Did he suppose she was going to become the next Virgin Mary? She glanced up and sobered at the serious look on his face.

Straightening in her seat, she stiffened her spine and her resolve, vowing not to let him get away with shunning the two children he already had.

"You have a son, remember? *He* is your heir." Her teeth hurt from gritting them. Andrew Wyatt was more than aware of the son he had, but chose to ignore. She hated him for that. In his eyes, females were worthless except for bearing their husbands males to further the family line and take over the business. Non-perfect males were to be kept in secret, banished as if they didn't exist.

That's exactly the way he'd treated her and her brother. Even more so when their mother abandoned them. Brianna had been just ten years old at the time, her brother, six months.

Her father threw a hand in the air. "Silence. That boy will never be able to do anything I need him to."

He would if you gave him the chance. Brianna seethed as she glared at him from beneath her lashes. Damn him to hell. Thank God she'd been able to shelter Scottie from most of the intense hatred and indifference running through their father's veins.

"So what, you expect me to get pregnant by some stranger just so you can have another penis in the house?" She couldn't stop her hands from clenching into white-knuckled fists.

"You'll do whatever I tell you to, if you ever want to see Scott again."

Ah, there it was. He'd played his trump card knowing she would do anything for Scottie. Anything for the "imperfect" baby boy who she'd single-handedly raised since his birth. In the dim interior of the limo, she could see the red fury of her father's face ebbing. A sure sign he knew he'd just won.

Her breath wheezed out of her lungs, a symptom of an impending asthma attack, as the delusional man sat across from her like a king on his throne.

A creak of leather as her father relaxed back into his seat refocused her attention. The redness of his jowls was gone now and a feral smile split his lips. What had he done?

"He's not a stranger anyway. He's Cole Masters." There was a triumphant gleam in his eyes.

Brianna barely refrained from laughing out loud and thought about what she knew about Cole Masters. He was in the top echelon of St. Louis's "Who's Who". He may even be the top. She'd overheard her father and his business partners speak of him often enough. He was rich beyond measure, many times over her father's own wealth, had a powerful corporate drive, and was way younger than most of his competitors.

He owned and lived on a prime piece of real estate which overlooked the Missouri River. The mansion itself had been scrutinized more than once for its architectural brilliance, having been designed by somebody famous, and had just recently been featured on the cover of a magazine.

As for the man himself, she had seen him many times in the media. He was a handsome, much coveted bachelor who regularly dated beautiful, sexy women. Women who fawned over him, batting their eyelashes and cooing like imbeciles. Women who had far more experience than Brianna could ever hope to have.

He was also rumored to have extravagant and shocking sexual tastes that ran from bondage to sharing. The gossip she'd heard through the grapevine had left her panties damp and her heart racing.

No, the gazillionaire would never agree to be a sperm donor.

Still, the mere thought of a man like Cole mastering her body and stroking her into oblivion made her stomach muscles clench. She crossed her legs in an effort to stave off the moisture pooling between her thighs, cringing when her now tight nipples sent an electric tingle throughout her body as they rubbed against the soft cotton fabric of her bra.

"If you're thinking you've just gotten out of this, it's already done," her father gloated.

Brianna's head snapped up, the blood rushing from her face.

"And stop that infernal noise you're making."

She fumbled in her pocket for her inhaler and somehow managed to give herself a puff despite her shakiness. Tears blurred her vision, though she couldn't decide if it was from wanting to laugh, or fright that he may have done something stupid. He could not be serious. This was the twenty-first century. Fathers did not give their daughters away to the highest bidder anymore. And daughters did not go willingly.

Cole Masters would laugh himself unconscious the second she walked through the door. Brianna would never measure up to his standard of women. She was five foot six and sometimes clumsy, not tall and graceful. She pulled her mouse-brown hair into a ponytail everyday and never let it fall in a cascading waterfall down her back. Her eyes were blue. Not cerulean, not Caribbean, not even sky. Just blue. She guessed her body was curvy and plump in all the right places, but no diet in the world would ever make her look svelte.

Her father sat taller and straightened his impeccable tie, indicating he was through talking to her. He pressed on the button which allowed communication with the driver.

"Where are you going?" Her stomach twisted in a knot, and for the second time she sorely wished she'd snubbed him and walked away.

"Not me. We. We're going to Cole's house. He's expecting you. Must you always dress like a slob?" he sneered.

Brianna lurched forward in her seat, strangling herself on the seatbelt in the process. "You cannot tell me who to have sex with!"

The fury returned to his face as he brought himself nose to nose with her and gripped her shoulders with fingers strong enough to crush her bones. "I'll damned well tell you who to fuck, and when, and if I have to hold you down while he does it, I will." Spittle shot from his mouth with his anger.

Brianna paled, the blood rushing from her brain and threatening to cause her to faint. "That's rape."

He shrugged. "If that's what you want to call it."

"You're insane. There's no way to even guarantee you'll get a boy!" How could she possibly get him to see reason?

Her father sat back again. He inspected his immaculately manicured nails as he spoke. "I am well aware of who controls the gender of a child, Brianna. Do not think to undermine my intelligence. Cole comes from a very long line of males. There's not a single, worthless female for five or more generations. I trust his sperm to do the right thing."

"I won't do it."

His bark of laughter quickly turned into a snarl as his hand snaked out to strike her cheek. It stopped just a breath away from her face.

"I would think you would not want Cole's first time meeting you to be hampered by a black eye or bloody lip, on top of your less than stellar looks. Surely you don't want his first impression of you to be one of an uncontrollable woman. After all, in a few short hours he's going to have his dick inside you, filling you with his remarkable DNA."

His words hit their mark and Brianna sank in her seat.

"Just think about Scott, all alone, without his precious sister protecting him. You'll never see him again, I promise." He leaned in close enough to where she could smell his whiskey-laden breath and her stomach turned over. His lip curled into a snarl. "As soon as you give me a son, you can pack both your things and Scott's, and get the hell out of my house."

Brianna trembled as tears slid down her cheeks. Her father didn't want a grandson. He planned to pass her baby off as his son! He didn't even want to keep her around as the baby's mother. She truly was just a vessel.

"Make yourself presentable, Brianna. You have forty-five minutes to do so." His tone brooked no argument.

She stared out the window of the limo and thought wildly about how to get out of the mess she was in.

"The doors cannot be opened from the inside, Brianna. I made certain of that earlier today." He spoke calmly now as if they were going to church, not to her scheduled rape. "Resign yourself to your fate, my dear. I'm sure if you do everything he tells you to, he'll go easy on you the first time."

He patted her knee like she was a child. Brianna jerked away from his touch and squeezed against the door, fresh tears falling with his snort of amusement. She could do this. For Scottie, she would do this horrible thing. She didn't think there was any chance of Cole agreeing, but they would soon find out.

* * *

"I'm telling you, Tyler, this guy's for real." Cole swung his feet up and settled them on top of his desk, then leaned back into his leather desk chair as he spoke on the phone to his security specialist and best friend, Tyler Cannon.

"Yeah, well," Tyler said, "I ran the check on him, and on her. No one seems to know much about her. The mother's not in the picture, hasn't been since Brianna was about ten. No one I talked to could tell me anything about Lydia Wyatt. I got the same story over and over. Apparently it was rare to see Lydia in public, but impressions were she was depressed. Some blue hair told me it might have been over a miscarriage. Anyway, one day she was there, the next day she was gone. Wyatt told everybody she went away to get help, but if she did, she never came back."

"There are no other children?"

"Sure, but none of them by his wife. Our boy likes to sleep around. A lot. I found four other kids, all girls, from different mothers, which he pays for on the side. Handsomely, I might add. Who knows how many more are out there."

Cole sighed and rubbed a weary hand over his face. "So what, is this Brianna ugly or something?"

"Not from the pictures I've seen. She's not beautiful by any stretch of the imagination, but there's something about her face. I got a hard-on looking at her."

"Well, that says it all right there."

Tyler laughed into the phone, and Cole laughed with him. The scary thing was, if Tyler got hard, then Cole would too. His cock thickened beneath the buttons of his worn jeans just thinking about the women they'd shared.

"I should get back early in the morning. I'll talk to you then and see how this meeting went. When's the holier-than-thou coming?" Tyler asked, his voice ringing with mockery.

"I'm waiting for him as we speak."

Tyler's grunt resonated through the phone. "And why exactly does he want this?"

"How the hell should I know? I told you, Freddy received this letter by courier late Friday evening. By the time I left Caroline—"

"When are you gonna see how big of a bitch she is," Tyler growled.

"Now see, that's why I never invite you."

"I wouldn't touch that vixen with a ten-foot pole. Someday she's gonna grab your balls, your money and your pride, and you'll never see 'em again.

"She'll never get the chance." Cole wondered how he'd lost this conversation with just the mention of Caroline. "By the time I got home, it was late, or early I guess. I opened it when I saw it sitting out on the desk. That's when I called you."

"And I do so appreciate you calling me in the dead of night. So what? You think he's planning on some kind of blackmail? Seems like a risky proposition, I'm not sure how he'd pull off getting any money out of this."

"That's why I pay you the big bucks. To find these things out."

"You've been paying me? I haven't seen any checks."

"No, but your company has." Cole pulled the phone off his ear and stared at it. Talking to Tyler was sometimes like talking to a two-year old.

"Temper, temper. Tell me again what the letter says. I get that the man wants an heir, but hell, he's got fuckin' five of 'em."

Putting the phone back to his ear, Cole heard a door slam and the honk of a horn. Tyler had been in his car then, probably staking out another one of his deadbeat dads. The man owned a multi-million dollar security company providing services for very well-off businesses and people, yet Tyler grew softhearted for any woman who needed help with her kids. Cole didn't even know how Tyler's name had become synonymous with I'll-find-your-ex-and-get-you-your-money, but somehow, word got around. About twice a month, Tyler would come to him, or simply call, and say he'd be back in a few days. Cole would wave him away, not needing to remind his best friend to keep in touch.

"The letter says, 'he is in need of a male heir to pass on his legacy'."

"Who talks like that?" Tyler barked.

Cole laughed. "You mean besides my own grandfather? Andrew Wyatt, I guess. Apparently he doesn't want his 'legacy' going to a girl. It doesn't seem likely the man will get it done by himself, seeing as he has five daughters with five different women."

"So why doesn't the dick just marry her off to the highest bidder?"

Cole shrugged, an action Tyler wouldn't see, but he felt the same way. "I don't know. If a man were to get her pregnant but not marry her, the baby's not a lot better off than the other four girls he's already got but doesn't acknowledge. I think the guy's a few barrels short of a brewery, if you ask me."

"A few barrels...what?" Tyler croaked.

"Never mind." Cole rolled his eyes. He tried to speak again, but his friend was laughing so hard Cole simply shook his head and hung up the phone.

A sharp knock on the door alerted him that his most honored guest was probably about to be announced.

"Master Cole, your guest has arrived."

"Thank you, Freddy. Make the bastard sweat for a few minutes, then show him in, will you?"

"Yes, Master Cole." The man nodded as he backed out of the room.

"Oh, and one more thing." Cole hid a grin behind the paper he was studying.

"Yes, sir."

"You are aware it's my last name that is Masters, not my first?"

"Yes sir, I am more than aware of that fact."

Cole lifted his gaze. They'd had this conversation a million times, but Freddy's straight-faced answer was always the same. "Okay, just making sure." He laughed out loud when the eighty-year-old man, who'd long ago become part of the family, made an abrupt turn on his heel and left the office, his shoes silent on the highly polished floor.

Freddy was completely aware of Cole's chosen lifestyle and sexual preferences. Sometimes he wondered if the man didn't get a kick out of calling him Master, even though Cole's tastes ran more to the pleasure of sharing a woman with Ty, than dominating.

His smile faded as his eyes dropped to the contract on the desk in front of him. Andrew Wyatt was actually trying to pawn his daughter off to be bred by some stranger like an animal.

He read the words again for about the fiftieth time, fighting both the nausea and the excitement warring inside him. On the one hand, his ego boosted to be chosen as a superior—Wyatt's word exactly—model for DNA. On the other, it made him sick to think a father had absolutely no morals where his daughter was concerned.

Tyler's background check on Andrew Wyatt had turned up exactly what Cole had feared. He had no ulterior motives, the bastard simply wanted to buy his sperm.

And what must Brianna be thinking? Were they both in on it? Did she know about him and what he liked? Did Wyatt know there was a chance any child born to his daughter might not be a Masters? Obviously not or Andrew wouldn't be contemplating this ridiculous scheme in the first place. Tyler was doing a fantastic job of keeping any number of rumors about them to just that. Rumors.

The door opened with a click and Cole stood and looked up dispassionately.

"Aah, Cole. Good to see you."

I wouldn't say the same.

Andrew Wyatt was dressed to impress in an Armani suit. Cole nearly laughed, as Wyatt took in his own mode of dress. Faded blue jeans, white T-shirt, and tennis shoes. A sharp contrast to the plush surroundings. The man's steps faltered.

"If you need more time to get ready, we can keep waiting."

Cole spread his arms. "You don't like what I'm wearing?" He sat back down, slouching in his chair, epitomizing the exact opposite of what a wealthy businessman should. Fuck him. He didn't owe this man anything, including respect. Wyatt didn't deserve any, either, whoring his daughter for the sake of an heir.

Wyatt's chin lifted. "It's not exactly appropriate for a business meeting."

Cole's nostrils flared along with his anger. "What business? You've come to my home, on Sunday, my day off, to offer your daughter like some sacrificial lamb." A whistling, wheezing noise caught Cole's attention. "What is that?"

Wyatt shifted and Cole glimpsed a small figure struggling behind him. He rose very slowly, counted to ten, and willed himself not to explode.

"Shut up, you imbecile," Wyatt snarled. The whistling grew louder.

Cole rounded his desk to get a better look, his anger growing by the second, praying the bastard had not brought his daughter along for this meeting. There could be no greater mortification. Unless she was into this sort of thing, which Cole doubted by the way she was shaking.

Wyatt's shoulder jerked rhythmically with each tug on his hand. The closer Cole got to him, the more Wyatt turned to shield the woman behind him. Cole feigned one direction, then darted to the other, successfully dodging behind the older man.

"Let her go, Wyatt." Cole's breathing nearly became as labored as Brianna's by what he saw. Her delicate wrists were manacled in her father's beefy fist, her hands nearly purple with the force of his grip. She gasped in and out, each breath wheezing with more force than the last. Cole was used to having a woman tied up, but not into manhandling. This produced only fear and pain, not the pleasure that was supposed to go along with being held tightly. He gritted his teeth and willed Brianna to look up at him.

A pair of very scared, startled sky-blue eyes finally peered at him from a pale heart-shaped face. Hair the color of a wheat field was tumbling out of her ponytail as she fought to be released.

The look on her face clawed at his heart, and yet his cock hardened to near bursting.

His thoughts raced to having her under him, his cock buried in her tight, wet heat, those eyes glazed over in passion, not fear. He imagined her on her knees, those thin, little wrists tied behind her back while she sucked him off.

"Jesus, must you make that hideous noise all the time?" The harsh words snapped Cole out of his fantasy. Wyatt flung Brianna away from him. She would have fallen to the ground had Cole not grabbed her as she stumbled backwards. "I hope you're proud of yourself…"

"Where's your inhaler?" Cole led her to the couch, concern gnawing at him. He knew instinctively she was having an asthma attack, having seen his little brother battle the disease for years.

"My p-poc-ket." She was dressed the same as he, butter-soft jeans and a pale blue T-shirt. He patted both the front and back pockets of her jeans, found it in the front, and dug two fingers in. He lowered her to the cushions and crouched in front of her. With one hand he held the inhaler to her lips, grimacing at the charge he got when her two wobbly hands gripped his forearm. His other hand went to the nape of her neck, caressing and calming.

His fingers missed nothing as he stroked her. The softness of her skin, the silkiness of her hair. Thank God he had the mental wherewithal to remember her father was still in the room, because he wanted to lean in and lick at the tender vee of her throat where her pulse beat erratically.

Again, he wondered how she would look when aroused and nearing an explosive climax only he, or Tyler, could give her. Her breathing jerked his mind out of the pleasure gutter.

"Come on, Bri, slow down, take a deep breath." His heart hammered as she tried to suck the albuterol into her lungs. "That's it, let the medicine work." Her eyes connected with his, both thankful and fearful, and Cole felt like he'd been kicked in the gut. Where the urge came from he didn't know, but he leaned forward and placed his lips on her forehead. At the same time, he delivered another puff of the medication.

Her body stiffened and then relaxed into the curve of his shoulder. Cole became aware Wyatt was still in his demeaning diatribe behind them, seemingly unaware of the trouble his daughter was having in fighting for a true breath.

"...Aww, isn't that sweet. You two have already hit it off. I apologize for this disgraceful episode."

She jerked in response to her father's words.

Cole remained in his squatting position and hissed over his shoulder. "Get the fuck out of my house, Wyatt."

Wyatt's mouth opened and closed like a fish, and a red stain crept up his thick neck. The man had obviously never had anyone give him a direct order before. Cole would make sure he knew who was in charge of this whole scenario, right now.

"You can't talk to me like that."

Cole passed his lips over Brianna's forehead once more and glimpsed an astonished look plastering itself to her delectable little face. Then he stood and faced a man who shouldn't be allowed to be a part of the human race.

"I'll talk to you any goddamn way I want to." He stabbed the egotistical bastard in the chest with his finger, another action Wyatt was clearly unused to. "This is my home, and you will not treat anyone within its walls with anything less than respect. Now get out." His teeth hurt he was gritting them so tightly.

"Wh-what about the contract? It has to b-be signed," Wyatt stammered.

Cole reached a hand around Wyatt's neck, grabbed the collar of his shirt, and squeezed the material in his fist. "You'll get your fucking contract in a week. No sooner." Cole twisted his arm so Wyatt was forced to turn around, and pushed the older man toward the door.

"So you'll do it? You'll get Brianna pregnant?"

"Oh, I'll do it all right." Cole's voice was deadly soft in the older man's ear.

Somehow, Wyatt seemed to miss the menace behind Cole's quiet words.

"Let's go, Brianna." Wyatt's voice was almost giddy with excitement.

"No. She stays with me." Cole ignored the gasp coming from the couch. "I don't want you anywhere near her until next Monday. You got that, *Mr.* Wyatt?"

*** *** ***

Brianna cringed when the door slammed, knowing how her father would react to a command. His face would darken, the vein at his temple would grow and pulse, and his nose would flare to the point you could lose a marble in one of his nostrils.

The two men continued to argue about their "arrangement" behind the closed door, although Brianna couldn't understand anything from the garbled but heated conversation.

She stared, shocked and dazed, at the floor and kept her hands fisted in her lap, fighting the urge to touch her forehead where Cole had slid his lips ever so gently over her skin. Twice. Her current panting had nothing to do with her asthma.

The man was gorgeous, with unruly, light brown hair framing his tanned face. His eyes were the color of the sky just before a storm, a sort of deep blue-gray. Beneath his T-shirt she had detected a flood of quivering muscles from his pecs to his abdomen. His jeans rode low on his lean hips, and even between gasps of shaky breath, Brianna had wanted to explore what was hidden underneath the snug denim.

Her heart thudded, aiding the rush of blood to volatile parts of her body. Her very utilitarian white cotton panties were damp. She squeezed her thighs together when a hint of her essence wafted to her nose, and closed her eyes, praying Cole wouldn't notice when he returned.

Maybe he wouldn't come back. He'd done his duty and played the white knight. Sympathy, tenderness and genuine concern had oozed from his pores, but had she seen any real interest on his part? And why would it offend her if she hadn't? She'd known from the start she would never be a temptation for him, no matter how eager she was to jump him.

This lustfulness was an alien feeling to her since she was hardly ever around men. Maybe it was a virgin's reaction to a mouthwatering body. Maybe her clock was ticking.

Didn't matter. She shook her head and contemplated why he had told her father he would go along with this stupidity.

And what had he meant when he'd said, "She stays with me"? She couldn't leave Scottie. There was no telling what her father would do to him if she wasn't home. Perhaps she could somehow convince Cole to help her. With what exactly? She nibbled her lip. Why would a gazillionaire help her with her brother? She didn't have anything to offer him in return. Or maybe she did, if the moisture between her legs was anything to go by. Of course, that would make her a whore.

She shuddered at the image of lying beneath Cole, naked as he touched her everywhere. She had to get out of here before her fantasies took over and she made a fool of herself in front of the richest man in St. Louis.

Brianna twisted and looked around the room for the first time. They had not gone up any steps, except those leading to the front door, so the ground couldn't be more than a few feet away. She launched herself off the pale leather couch where

Cole had seated her and dashed to the wall of windows opposite her.

She yanked on the cord controlling the blinds and sucked in a frantic breath when the oak-colored wood slats shot upward with an alarming racket. Her gaze flew to the door and held for longs seconds. When it didn't open, the breath she was holding whooshed out of her lungs.

Disappointment soared as she looked out on the immaculate courtyard. It was a gigantic adult-sized play land, complete with tennis court, swimming pool, trampoline, putting green and bar. Beyond that, in the distance, was a spectacular view of the valley containing the Missouri River.

The problem was that the estate was a walkout and she was at least ten feet, if not more, above the ground. Heights had never been good for her.

God, she wished she'd taken those yoga classes years ago. Some relaxation techniques would be good right about now. If ever there was a more desperate situation to get out of, the time was now.

"Just close your eyes," she mumbled and attacked the latch.

"Going somewhere?" The deep, amused voice rumbled from behind her.

Brianna spun around, a guilty flush staining her cheeks. Cole Masters lounged in the doorway. The door she hadn't heard open. His feet were crossed at the ankle, his arms across his chest. A lock of hair had fallen over his eye, and she itched to brush it away. A mischievous grin played at his incredibly sexy mouth. He could have been the model for the "David".

Brianna licked her suddenly dry lips. Cole's face tightened and took on a look of what she could only describe as hunger.

"Why are you here?" He was blunt, if nothing else. He shoved his body off the doorframe and stalked toward her.

How much should she tell him?

"Why would a beautiful, young woman bow down to a crazy man?" He held up his hand just as she opened her mouth. "He is crazy, Bri. No sane man would whore his daughter for the sake of an heir."

She gulped as he drew closer to her body, his hips swaggering, drawing her eyes to the very yummy region of his body. He'd used the exact word she had in describing her situation. Whore.

She straightened, determined he would not see her as a cowering little girl who did everything her father told her to do. She'd never done so before, mostly because he'd never asked anything of her, and she wasn't going to start now. Somehow, she'd find a way to protect Scott and get out of this ridiculous arrangement.

Besides, she could give as well as he could. "Why are *you* doing this?"

Cole snorted, startling her, and shrugged carelessly. "I can't even begin to imagine why. I was ready to throw your old man out the door when I saw you struggling behind him. Now you've peaked my interest, and to be honest, there's something about you I can't resist."

"What?"

He leaned in close to her face, and whispered, "You want me."

"I do not." The lie sounded pathetic even to her.

He squashed her lips with a lean forefinger and nodded. "Yes, you do. I could read it in you the minute I laid eyes on you. You just don't know it yet."

Didn't she? Hadn't she had dreams of being tied up and screaming with pleasure as a man took her? This man.

Brianna swallowed. He sounded so tender, not demanding the way her father did. He began to slowly circle her, his arm never breaking contact with her body. She shivered in response as he grazed along her back and shoulder blades, then to her front where he passed by her breasts. Her nipples stood at attention, straining against the fabric of her bra and T-shirt.

Cole leaned back and stared at his handiwork.

Instinct kicked in and Brianna crossed her arms over herself to cover her body's reaction to his simple touch.

"Never." Cole reached out and grasped her hands, tugging gently to dislodge her arms. "Never cover yourself with me." His gravelly voice demanded obedience, but didn't even raise an octave. Brianna found herself wanting to obey anything he asked.

"Were you running away?"

The change of subject shocked her, dispelling the intimate sizzle she had just experienced as quickly as it had come. She blinked, returning to reality.

"Answer me, Bri." His fingers caressed her arm from elbow to wrist and back again.

Her eyes popped, her hands fisted. Lifting her chin, she finally answered. "Yes, I was running." How could she possibly stay here? Scottie. For Scottie she would have to find a way. She would not let her father send him to an institution. Again she thought of simply asking Cole to help.

"By jumping out the window?" He shrugged as if the whole idea was crazy and stepped closer, his sweet breath tickling her nose. "Seems kind of dangerous to me."

"Yeah, well, I can't imagine you, of all people, would want to have anything to do with sharing your sperm with me so my father can have an heir."

Cole raised an eyebrow. "Me, of all people?"

"Yes you. You know, you being so rich and good looking. You could have anyone. And probably have." She muttered the last words under her breath.

He grinned. An honest to goodness, very boyish grin. Brianna slurped the drool back into her mouth.

"You think I'm good looking?"

She rolled her eyes. "Oh, please. Save me from male egos." She stepped away from him only to have him advance on her again.

"Do not back away from me, Bri."

There was that sensual, implacable voice again. She closed her eyes, savoring it, nearly moaning at the gush of cream flooding her crotch.

His mouth tickled at her ear. "I can smell your arousal, Bri. I know how turned on you are by me. By the thought of us together."

He pressed into her, effectively trapping her between the wall at her back and his delectable body. His cock was hard against her much softer belly. She groaned and dropped her head to his chest, unable to break the spell he was casting on her.

"I know why your father brought you here. What I can't understand is why you, an adult woman, would come willingly. Or is it just you thought you could get a piece of me?"

The air hissed through her lungs when she sucked in a breath. "Do you want the truth?"

"No, I like it when my blackmailers lie to me." The sarcasm dripped from his perfect lips. The perfect lips just inches from her own. The lips that pressed against her, asking for more, the tip of his tongue rubbing along the seam of her mouth.

She gasped as his words sank into her mushy, lust-filled mind and broke the contact. "Black... My father's paying you. If anyone is being blackmailed here, it's me."

Cole's face twisted in disbelief.

"It's true," she insisted.

Annmarie McKenna

He folded his arms over his chest, tucked his chin, and peered at her from beneath lashes long enough to make any woman jealous. His eyes clearly shouted, "Yeah, right."

Time to come clean.

"Okay, the whole truth."

"And nothing but," he said gruffly.

She swallowed. "He threatened to put my brother in an institution if I don't go through with this ridiculous scheme."

"Brother?" he shouted. "There was no mention of a brother." He ground his hands over his face. "Try a different story."

Brianna's mind whirled. "What do you mean, no mention? You had me followed," she said in sudden realization. "You knew all about this and were willing to go along with it?"

"Hell no. And yes, I did a background check so I could have all the facts before I was blackmailed."

"But, I already told you, I'm the one being—"

"Yeah, yeah." He waved her off. "I know, you're the victim here."

"Clearly." She was sooo pissed. How dare the man think she would have something to do with this.

"So, please keep telling me your lie, I mean, the truth."

"Oh, you are so gonna feel bad when you see for yourself I'm telling the truth." She would have liked to smack the arrogant beast, but he still had her pinned to the wall. She had no chance whatsoever of getting a good angle on him. And was it just her imagination, or had his penis gotten even bigger?

"Like I said, I have a brother, Scottie, well Scott. He was born when I—"

"Wait a minute," he interrupted. "If you have a brother, why in the hell does daddy need an heir so bad."

"If you'd let me finish, I'll tell you."

"Sorry."

He didn't look or sound the least bit sorry. She cleared her throat. "He was born when I was ten."

"So he's what, sixteen?"

She growled as he interrupted yet again. "Yes. During the labor, and right after, he had a series of small strokes. They left him blind and deaf in his right ear. Anyway, my *daddy* thought he would never be good enough to continue the business." She lifted her chin. "I've been raising Scottie from day one."

"So Scott is a secret? Which explains why Tyler didn't find anything on him."

Aah, now the man was catching on. She nodded. "Who's Tyler? And yes, a secret. My father hates that his only son isn't perfect. If he'd only spend a tiny amount of time with him, he'd see what a great man he's going to turn into. Physical limitations and all."

She started to get excited. She loved talking about her brother, not that there were many people to whom she could talk about him. Especially since she was never allowed to mention him. Her father would kill her if he could hear her now. "I've been home-schooling him. Scottie is really smart, extremely lonely, but very intelligent. You'd like him, he's a great kid."

"You love him, don't you?" Cole's words were laced with compassion.

"Yeah, I do." She sighed, letting her shoulders relax half an inch. "He's why I'm here. My father asked me if I would go for a ride with him, something he'd never done before. Curious, I said yes, and that's when he dropped this little bombshell. I tried to make him see reason, that there was no way to guarantee anyone could give him a boy. But he laughed and said he'd researched your family and there hasn't been a girl born for generations."

"Hmm. I guess he didn't research well enough, or he would have known I'm adopted."

Brianna choked and then, ridiculously, started giggling.

Cole's left eyebrow arched. "You find that funny?"

His mouth brushed across her cheek, making her shiver. "No, no, not at all. It's just...he's such a planner, and this will really tick him off."

"Oops." He shrugged as his knuckle traced lightly over the cheek he'd just kissed.

She sagged against his lean body, trembling from his touch and wanting more. "So, what do we do now?"

"We go along with it."

"Why would we do that? Why would you hand over your sperm," her face burned as she said the words, "knowing you'd never have a say in your child's life. That's despicable."

"Let's get one thing straight here. I won't ever 'hand over' any of my sperm for your father's use. I will, however, share it for my own use." He shrugged again, an action she was getting very used to.

Brianna snapped her head backward, smacking it on the wall and dazing herself. She squeezed her eyes shut. This could not be happening.

"Jesus." Cole's voice was gruff and laced with the same earlier concern for her well-being. "You're going to be hell for me to keep healthy, aren't you?"

His hands tenderly rubbed the bump forming on the back of her skull. He lowered his head until their foreheads touched.

"I think I want to leave now." She forced the words out while her brain and heart were both shouting, *No you don't you little idiot. You want to ease this insistent ache between your legs.* She had a feeling only Cole could do that for her.

Cole chuckled. "No you don't."

His right hand slid down her cheek, her jaw line, her neck, over her heart, and came to rest on her left breast. Her traitor of a nipple stabbed his palm as he kneaded the soft mound of flesh that had never before known a man's hand.

"What you really want is for me to fuck you."

"No," she denied, shaking her head.

"You want me to suck these hard, tight, little nipples."

"No." She shook her head harder. He pressed more fully into her, his thigh rubbing against her swollen clit. A groan slid past her lips as he kissed around her face while he talked.

"You want me to tie you down, your legs spread wide. You want me to go down on you, to stab my tongue inside you, to suck on your clit until you explode in my mouth."

His hands slid slowly south and eased under the hem of her shirt. Her tummy muscles quivered as fingers stroked her abdomen on their way back north. Then they were at her bra, flicking the clasp between her breasts open and easing the material off her plumpness.

He was killing her! The tips of his fingers skated across the top of the breasts he'd just uncovered, learning them through unseen touch. Brianna sagged against the wall, her head rolling back and forth on the hard surface with the exquisite feelings he invoked.

Dimly she realized the only thing holding her up was his thigh, which she was subconsciously grinding her mound against. He sucked her earlobe into the moist heat of his mouth and nibbled gently with his sharp teeth.

"Come for me, Bri," he whispered.

She exploded and screamed and dropped her cheek to his shoulder. He pinched her nipple between his fingers and rolled it gently as her climax ebbed beneath his assault.

God! How humiliating. She had come at his command. She loved this man and she'd known him less than an hour. No. Not love, lust. She lusted after him. It wasn't possible to love someone in such a short amount of time.

At some point he'd removed his hand from her shirt and hugged her closer to him. His chin rested on top of her head.

Embarrassed, Brianna hid her face in his chest. She felt like the whore she'd thought about earlier, coming like that. Surely he'd throw her out the door now. The thought panicked her in more ways than one. If she didn't stay, Scottie would be taken away *and* she'd never see Cole again.

The second she got her breathing under control, Cole lifted her face with the crook of his finger. He stared at her, like he was looking into her soul, then he descended on her and kissed her with what felt like everything he had. His lips melded with hers, prying them easily apart and his tongue thrust between her teeth. It stroked her own with velvet softness, teaching her how he wanted to be kissed back. He sucked her tongue into his mouth and held it with a strong suction. Brianna felt her arms lift to cling around his neck.

The kiss was over before she wanted it to be, and Cole was backing off, standing her on her own two feet and steadying her with his hands at her shoulders. Brianna licked her lips, tasting him again and wishing he were still there.

Cole chuckled, bringing a flood of color to her face, then sobered into an intense stare. "I want you, Brianna, there's no denying that. And based on your response, you want me too. So here's the deal. I'll give your brother anything he needs if you stay and do anything I ask you to." His eyes glinted with mischief. "Sexually, of course."

Her knees nearly buckled. She could not have heard him right. He would help her brother in exchange for her body. "My body for my brother? Sounds like another round of blackmail to me." Not to mention she was afraid she would lose more than control of her body. Somehow she felt her heart would be involved.

"Mm. You can take it that way. But make no mistake. I don't just want your body, I want all of you. Meaning you would do anything I say, no questions asked."

She must have looked seriously bewildered because he added, "There'll be plenty of time for me to explain later." He turned, leaving her staring helpless at his back. "For now I'll show you to your room."

Uncertain about his abrupt change in demeanor, Brianna stood, unmoving. As if he hadn't just given her an earth-shattering climax, Cole turned to her and held out a hand. He looked certain she would come to him. She did, as if pulled by some magic string, clasping his hand and somehow trusting him with her life for at least the next week.

Chapter Two

Cole pulled the only slightly reluctant Bri behind him, the pounding of his heart echoing in his ears. He couldn't wait to take her completely and make her his. She already was his, if the size of his hard-on had anything to say about it.

He didn't know what had prompted him to offer refuge for her younger brother. He only knew he had to have her. Some innate sense told him she would fit nicely between Tyler and himself. A woman who would be perfect for both of them. It was scary how strong the feeling was, making it hard to think about anything but how she would look and the noises she would make, as he and Ty pumped their erections in and out of her.

Cole paused outside his master suite, sure Bri would balk at staying in his room and in his bed, but he was not about to give her any breathing room. Well, actually he was. After booting her father out the door, he'd called his physician to come and give her a complete evaluation. She probably wouldn't like that either, but he was getting increasingly concerned about her asthma.

Had her father ever had her monitored or tried other medications? From what he'd seen and heard from the bastard, he didn't think so. Cole would take it upon himself to see she received anything she needed or wanted. She'd already affected him that much.

"I'll have your things sent over and brought in here," he told her as he tugged her through the door. He knew what she would see. An imposing four-poster bed. Each post was adorned with various rings and hooks. *The better to tie you up with, my dear.* Most of the other furniture was standard issue and functional.

"Is this *your* room?" Her voice was trembling, he hoped from the bliss he'd just launched her into, and not fear.

"Yes. My room, my bed." He turned to her. "We'll be spending a lot of time here, Bri." For now he'd wait to tell her about Tyler. He watched her bite her lip, probably wondering if she'd made the right decision or not. Her vulnerability made him want her even more, and he blatantly adjusted his cock in his jeans to show her just how he felt. Her eyes widened in what Cole read as shocked curiosity.

"Why don't you get comfortable? Take a bath, rest, whatever. I'll have Freddy send up a tray of snacks for you. The doctor will be here in a couple of hours." He nearly laughed at the look on her face and would have had she not also looked so scared. He caressed her cheek with his knuckles, wanting to feel the softness of her skin again. They flushed prettily under his ministration. With his thumb he rubbed at her bottom lip where she'd bitten it and nearly groaned out loud when he thought about those lips wrapped around his cock.

"Why? So you can see if I'm childbearing worthy?" she demanded, yanking him out of his fantasy.

"I wouldn't give a shit if you could never have children," he growled. "I called because I don't like the sound of your asthma, Bri. Have you seen your doctor lately?" Cole watched as her breathing sped up just thinking about it.

"No." She swallowed and her gaze darted around the room. He could tell she was waging a battle within herself not to cry.

"Why not? Asthma is not something to play around with." At her questioning look, Cole lifted a shoulder. "My little brother's got it. I've helped him for years get through some pretty scary attacks."

"That's nice."

He raised an eyebrow in disbelief. "You're the last person who should think having to battle this disease is nice."

"No, no. Not that. You really don't need to go to all that trouble for me." She backed away from him and he thought he saw her flinch. Did she think he would hit her? Had her father?

Okay, he probably would be doing some hitting, but not in anger. He would cut off his arm before he'd hurt the doe-like creature standing in front of him.

"I just meant, it's nice, that...that you, you know, helped him. Get through it I mean."

"No one's ever been there for you?" He advanced on her, took her hands and rubbed her knuckles with his thumbs.

"Helga did once, but my father fired her when his dinner was late. She'd taken me to the emergency room because I couldn't stop coughing, even with my inhaler."

She said this matter-of-factly as though it weren't an unusual occurrence for the staff to be fired for showing an interest in the man's daughter.

He cursed beneath his breath. "How old were you?"

"Eleven."

"Jesus. Well," he cleared his throat, "I don't want to have to worry about you fighting for a breath while you're fighting for an orgasm."

He laughed when she yanked her hands out of his, but grabbed her chin with his thumb and forefinger.

"Seriously. I want you healthy."

Bri took on a mutinous look. "So you can stuff me with your sperm to provide my father with an heir?" Her face was beginning to burn red.

So there was some fire underneath her shyness after all. Too bad someone had given her such an ugly version of how sex with a man would be. One guess who that was. No matter, he'd change her opinion really quick.

He sighed. "How many times are you going to bring that up? I thought we already agreed we'd do this for us and your brother, not your father. I promise that my sperm, should they happen to congregate with one of your eggs, will never benefit Andrew Wyatt other than possibly making him a grandfather."

"Ever heard of a condom? A thin sheet of rubber would keep your sperm from going to church with my eggs. Then we could just say it didn't work."

She looked so hopeful staring up at him and nibbling on her lower lip. He wanted to push her to her knees and have her use those teeth on his dick. His naked dick. Asinine as it was he wanted Bri skin to skin, nothing between them but her slick juices coating them both as he slid in and out of her.

He growled at the image. "I have never had sex without a condom. Never." He pushed her bangs off her forehead and caressed an eyebrow with his thumb. "There's something about you, Bri, and God help me, I don't know why, but I don't want there to be anything between us the first time I take you. And I will take you, baby. Soon." She shivered when he replaced his thumb with his lips.

He resisted the urge to shiver himself. He'd never been affected by a woman this way.

"I'm just having a hard time with this whole thing. I don't know anything about you and you don't know anything about me. I feel like I'm being used."

She sounded incredulous, and he watched as she continued to chew on her lip, anxiety mixed with a certain amount of curiosity. He wondered if she were somehow trying to justify wanting him by voicing as many concerns as possible, most of them dealing with not wanting to provoke her father and possibly losing her tenuous hold on Scott.

"I am a twenty-six-year-old woman, not an object you can throw away when you're done with me. Especially not if we're going to have unprotected sex," she hissed.

Especially not if we're going to have sex, she'd said. He felt like pumping his fist in the air like a horny teenager out to get his first lay. He'd forget about the unprotected part. If she was okay with it, that's all that mattered.

"Believe me, I know you're a woman, but let's get one thing straight here. You have an ulterior motive for being here or you would have walked long ago. And I told you, if your brother's that important to you, then I will do anything to get him over here where he'll be safe." He let his hand drift again to stroke her nipple and was rewarded when her head fell back and her eyes closed on a moan. He kissed the exposed column of her throat. "And I will use you." He kissed around her face. "But, I would never throw you away." Her head came back up, shock registering on her face, but he couldn't take back the words he'd just said.

He didn't know why they'd slipped from his lips, but they felt right.

"But you're still going to try and give my father what he wants?"

"No, not try. But what your father doesn't realize is if a child is created between us," *the three of us, that is,* "I would never allow it to be separated from me." His voice was stern but he made sure the hand resting at her throat was gentle. Her nostrils flared with each breath and he was close enough his lips brushed hers as he spoke again. "What he also doesn't realize is that I would never separate my children from their mother."

Her gaze shot to his eyes, ripped from their spot watching his lips. Before she could even think about speaking, Cole turned her around and patted her butt. With a small shove, he propelled her toward the bathroom.

"Go, bathe. We'll talk later. About everything."

With a very confused glance over her shoulder, Bri padded toward her immediate destiny, proving once again that, subconsciously at least, she trusted him.

His cock grew even further as he watched the sway of her slightly flared hips. None of his previous lovers, make that partners, had affected him the way Bri did. For God's sake, she had sat on his thigh and ridden him like the untrained virgin she was and then came at his command.

Walking back to his office, he smiled remembering the scene. Once his position was established more firmly, he would have her eating out of his hand, literally, and coming as he or Tyler demanded, all the time. It would be a pleasure to train her in the fine art of fucking. It was what she wanted, he had seen it in her eyes the moment she'd looked up at him the first time.

He'd confirmed his suspicions later when she'd exploded around his leg, squeezing his thigh with her own and screaming like a banshee. She had said no twice, but hadn't meant it. The glazed look in her eyes had said, *Please God, if you don't fuck me, I'll die.*

Somewhere deep inside her was a sensuality she hadn't tapped into yet. Tyler and he would find it and exploit it in no time. He had a feeling once they got started she'd be begging them for more. Especially if being with the two of them meant she could keep her brother safe and not return to Andrew Wyatt.

The man was a first-class bastard. Cole snarled. He could only imagine what Bri had endured at her father's hands.

With the two of them, Bri would be cherished. Probably put on a pedestal if Tyler had anything to say about it. The man had a way with women which left even the oldest of grandmothers drooling.

Tyler, as the security specialist, had quickly made the first rumors surrounding their sharing just that. A rumor, a fantasy. Something one woman made up to make her friends jealous, which couldn't be corroborated. Since then, the only women they shared were the ones less inclined to talk about their sexual escapades because they felt they had something to lose. Mostly their status in society.

In his house, in his arms, Bri would know pleasure and pain. The sweet kind of pain specifically designed to bring her to a screaming orgasm. A pleasure he would feed off for his own. Come next Monday, she wouldn't want to return to her father's house. And suddenly, he didn't want her to. He wanted to keep her, to find out what made her tick, to get under her skin and make her melt like putty in his hands. Right now, what he most wanted was to fuck her unconscious and then take her again.

His fisted his hands at his sides, his cock near exploding. He'd take her soon enough. Again and again, until all she could think about was him filling her pussy.

** ** **

Brianna luxuriated in the huge whirlpool tub, letting the powerful jets soothe her tired muscles. Today had been a day from hell. She felt like she was caught in a dream—except her tub at home had never made her feel this good. She wondered what Scottie was doing right now and about the offer Cole had put on the table.

Her brain shifted back and forth. How did she get out of this predicament, but then, did she really want to? She sighed, thinking about the things Cole had promised with his mouth, hands and eyes.

She didn't relish becoming one of his many conquests, but remembering the earlier earth-shattering orgasm he'd given her had her thinking. Who in their right mind would give up an opportunity to make love to the gorgeous man? Despite all the rumors she'd heard about him. If he could truly help her keep Scottie safe from her father, why would a little sex matter? It was the part about giving herself completely to him that had her worried.

Her nipples hardened as she pictured herself tied up, at his mercy.

Brianna slid a hand down her slick, water-heated body and settled on the tight little nub nestled in her pubic hair. She sighed with contentment as her middle finger circled her clit and she relaxed deeper into the tub, letting the water swirl and bubble around her chin.

She imagined Cole behind her, his arms encircling her, his hands gliding over body. With a finger and thumb, she teased a nipple, pinching and rolling it, adding to the building sensations.

Her back arched as his finger slid deep inside her pussy, drawing out her cream. In minutes, she was near the brink and vaguely aware of the water sloshing out to splash on the shiny, marble floor. A scream shattered the humid air of the bedroom-sized bathroom. Dimly, Brianna realized she was the one making all the noise.

The door flew open and smacked against the wall behind it. Brianna yelped, surprised by the sudden intrusion. Instinct had her submerging beneath the water in mortification.

She hadn't taken a good breath, and her already unhealthy lungs could no longer support her without any air. She came back up, breaking the surface of the water and blowing off the bubbles gathered on her nose.

"Are you all right, miss? Shall I go get Master Cole?"

"No," Brianna sputtered. Having him see her like this would be the ultimate in humiliation. "I'm fine."

The maid placed a hand over her heart. "Phew. I brought in a tray of goodies. Cole said you might be hungry after your ordeal this morning."

She fairly danced as she went about tidying the bathroom and mopping the flooded floor with a towel, uncaring about the naked woman in her "Master's" tub.

"You scared me with all that screaming. Cole told us you have really bad asthma and that we should keep an eye on you."

If I were having an attack, I wouldn't be able to scream, lady. She hated feeling like she was being treated with kid gloves. First Cole and now his staff. No, she realized. She wasn't being fair. They were concerned about her, that's all.

Better warn the maid off before Cole fired the poor girl for spending too much time with her. It was hard to tell someone to get lost when you were naked and just barely covered in quickly popping bubbles. She cleared her throat, ready to send the giddy young woman away, when Cole burst through the door.

"What happened?" he demanded.

He was breathing heavy like he'd just run up ten flights of stairs, or maybe just one and then a long hallway. Her face heated again, betraying her guilt at getting caught with her hand in the proverbial cookie jar. It was a detail Cole saw immediately. His nostrils flared, his lips curled, and he emitted a low growl Brianna was certain only she heard because she was so focused on him.

* * *

"Leave us, Rachel."

Startling at his tone, the maid bustled out the door with a mumbled, "Yes, sir."

Heedless of her nudity, Brianna, a panicked look on her face, rose to her knees and held out her hands. "Please, don't be angry, Cole. She heard me scream and came to check on me, I swear."

Remembering her story about Helga, Cole sighed. He grabbed both her hands and squeezed them between his own.

"Bri, I would never fire one of my staff for befriending you. I'm more likely to do so if they shunned you, but that won't happen. Now," he said, unable to hide his smile at her stunned look, "what am I going to do about the fact that you climax *very* loudly?"

She gasped and struggled to regain her hands, no doubt in an attempt to cover her perfect little body.

"Ah, ah. No covering up, remember? Your body is mine, for as long as you're with me. Mine to do with as I wish." He watched her swallow, turned on by his words. "As much as I love hearing how you feel, there will be some rules."

"I haven't said I would do this yet."

She sounded defiant, but not unwilling. He ignored her comment.

"Your first lesson." He stared into her eyes, wanting her full attention to be on him, and not visions of their future interactions. "You will not touch yourself unless I tell you to. If I am not with you, you will keep your itchy little fingers occupied elsewhere." He punctuated his words with a kiss to each of her fingers. "Do you understand?"

Her eyes went wide with shock, or perhaps indignation. He watched a battle ensue within them, knowing who would win, and was rewarded with a silent nod.

"Stand up and step out of the tub." He assisted her shaky body, when what he wanted to do was scoop her up, plant her against the wall and slide his cock inside her bath-warmed softness, knowing he would find her pussy drenched from her recent ministrations.

He turned her to face the mirror and stepped behind her. Once again Bri lifted her arms and tried to cross them, her cheeks red as he looked at her reflection. Cole grabbed her hands and pulled them behind her back, forcing her delectable rosy-tipped breasts out.

"When I release your hands, you will let them hang at your sides. If you move them again, I will punish you. Do you understand?"

He smiled when she licked her lips and swallowed, in fear or anticipation, he wasn't sure.

He brushed her hair away, gaining access to the sweet skin of her neck. Over her shoulder he could see the tight buds of her breasts. "I love it when you say my name." He reached around her with his right hand and fondled her breast, kneading the soft tissue in his larger hand and rolling the nipple in his fingers, pulling it gently away from her body.

Brianna sighed and her head fell back against his chest. He chuckled at her easy arousal.

"Your mouth looks like a kiss when you say Cole. It makes me think about how those lips will look as they kiss my cock and suck it into your sweet little mouth." Her knees buckled, and he caught her with both his arms around her, his hands still at her breasts. "Stand, Bri."

She stood, wobbly, and he nestled himself firmly in the small of her back. The image of her mouth on him had him straining against the buttons of his fly. He turned her to face him and crooked her face with his finger, checking to make sure her eyes were really full of lust, even though he could smell her arousal coming off her in waves. She wanted this, there was no doubt in his mind.

"Get on your knees, Bri, with your back straight, your thighs spread about a foot apart."

Her eyes widened and she swallowed, but ultimately, if not slowly, did what he asked of her. He liked how her spine stiffened with a tiny bit of defiance. That was good. It wasn't his aim to strip away her pride.

"Unbutton my jeans and pull them down to my knees."

He could see her mouth watering at the thought, and the tip of her pink tongue darted out to moisten her lips. He nearly groaned out loud but held back, not wanting to give any hint he could lose control, or that all along, she would be the one with all the control.

Her tentative hands reached for his fly. They were vibrating, and he wondered briefly if she'd be able to undo the buttons. But then, just as her fingertips caressed his bulging cock, nearly sending him to his knees, her hands steadied and fastened on the top of his jeans.

He sucked in a breath as her delicate fingers pushed the first button through its hole and then went to work on the next. Her fingernails scraped against the straining head of his cock as they pulled on the fabric, causing a drop of pre-come to moisten the slit.

"That's it, Bri, keep going. My cock is begging to be released, to be held in your tight little fist, licked by that velvet tongue of yours."

* * *

His words strengthened her resolve and Brianna attacked the next button. With that released, the top of his cock popped out, its large, purpled head shiny with nature's lubricant. Bri stared at it, mesmerized by its size and color. It was smooth as a baby's butt, and she ached to know all about it.

"Lick it," he growled.

Cole had read her thoughts. She leaned forward, sticking her nose right in his crotch, and inhaled his heady scent. A mixture of musk and man. She reveled in the sight of him, hard as steel for her, a virgin with very little knowledge about sex. She had a feeling that was about to change. For some reason, Cole Masters was hungry for her.

She jumped when he grabbed her roughly by the back of her head, tangling his fingers in her hair, just to the point of pain. To her surprise, her pussy wept. She felt it drip on her leg. It excited her.

"Lick it now, Bri."

Not sure how or where he wanted her to lick the head of his cock, she stuck the tip of her tongue out and did what looked the most pleasing to her. She ran it along the slit of his penis, lapping up the glistening drop of fluid and tasting its saltiness. His belly quivered and tightened above her head in reaction.

"Again."

This time she used the flat of her tongue to sweep across the broad head, soaking it in her saliva.

He pulled her away, apparently satisfied with her attempts at licking him, and motioned for her to continue taking his jeans off. Excited now, she made quick work of the rest of the buttons and greedily shoved the denim off his hips to his knees where he'd indicated.

His cock sprung free, huge and glorious, and obviously wanting in attention. It was thick and smooth with a heavy vein running the length of it underneath. Her heart jumped in fear, wondering how he thought she could possibly take the massive penis inside her. She shuddered.

A pull on her hair had her looking at him, and Brianna could see he had recognized her anxiety.

"I'll fit, I promise. Whichever part of you I decide to take, it'll fit perfectly."

That statement made her breath catch. She hadn't thought of that. He, being who he was, would intend to fuck her in places other than her pussy. God, she was so naïve. Heat pooled low in her belly and her clit clenched at the thought of him pumping in and out of her anus.

"Take me in your mouth, Bri. All of me."

Her eyes widened. It wasn't possible, despite his reassurances. Still, she leaned into him. She reached out with her hands to steady herself on his thighs and brought her lips around the large head of his cock.

"Jesus," he whispered.

Just as her tongue came out to meet his soft skin, he thrust into her mouth. She stilled, shocked by his penetration. Her mouth was shoved full, his cock buried against the back of her throat. She gagged and tried to back away, panic setting in, but he held her head to him with his big hand, forcing her to accept his cock.

"Relax your throat, Bri. You can do this, it's mind over matter. You can still breathe through your nose, I'm not choking you."

She begged her brain to think about what he was saying and a few seconds later, she stopped squirming and took her first breath through her nose.

He was right. She could still breathe, and though the gag reflex was still making itself known, he wasn't hurting her in any way. She reveled in that, and swallowed around his cock, trying to get rid of the vast amount of saliva pooling in her mouth with her panic.

Brianna heard Cole's teeth grinding together and when he told her to "do that again," he spoke through clenched teeth. His response excited her further, so she swallowed a second time.

Suddenly his cock was gone, pulled nearly out of her mouth, then was back, sliding all the way in before retreating once more.

"Tighten your lips and suck me as I move in your mouth, baby."

She did so without hesitation, wanting more than anything to please him. His pubic hairs tickled her nose each time he dove in, and her head stung where he pulled at her hair, but her pussy was dripping with want.

She found herself desperately wanting to touch her clit, knowing the smallest amount of provocation would have her screaming. Her hand moved, but at the last second she remembered his warning to never touch herself without his permission.

Her hands clenched into fists, but she obeyed his command, pleasing him more of a turn on than making herself come right now.

"Get ready for my come, Bri. Swallow me."

His voice was gruff, and at first she rebelled, not wanting to swallow something she knew nothing about, but before she could shake her head in denial or pull away, he thrust deep in her throat and growled above her.

Hot, wet jets of liquid shot into her mouth, and she had no choice but to swallow. It was that or drown, she thought wildly. The pumping seemed endless, and she sucked at him with vigor, milking him dry. She never thought she would do something like that, but she'd actually savored his taste on her tongue, and had not been revolted, as she thought she might. She kept her lips so tight around him, the head of his cock made a popping sound when he pulled it from her mouth.

"Fuck," he said and ran a hand through his hair.

Brianna sat back on her haunches, wiping at her mouth where a mixture of spit and semen had pooled, waiting for whatever Cole asked of her. Her arousal wafted up to her nose, reminding her she'd been left out of their little party.

"Christ, Bri, you're a fucking natural at that."

The statement made her proud and excited. It was a heady feeling knowing she had the ability to bring Cole pleasure. He, who only dated the most beautiful of beautiful women and could own damn near half the state. For him to say those words to her, a peon to him, made her feel like a goddess.

Cole pulled Brianna up and kissed her. His tongue emulated his cock and plundered her still come-coated mouth. She was breathless when he finally broke the kiss and pressed his forehead against hers.

"You want to feel my mouth on your pussy?"

She wanted that so bad, it was all she could do to not jump up and down and beg, but how easy would that make her look? Indecision battled inside her for about two seconds. "Yes, Cole."

* * *

He squeezed her in a bear hug. "Don't ever let me catch you telling me something you think I want to hear. I'd have known you were lying just then, if you'd told me something stupid like, no. I would have punished you for it too."

Her eyes grew big and Cole knew he'd hit the head on the nail. She had contemplated not telling him yes. For the most part, he wanted her to beg for release. It made the explosion that much sweeter, to be held off until the last possible second, but he wouldn't deny her now after what he'd just experienced. Bri had given him the best fucking blowjob he'd ever had, bar none. And she'd never done it before.

"Get on the bed and lay on your back with your arms stretched above your head and your legs spread wide."

She swallowed, a habit he was quickly learning was her nervousness showing through. He knew she wouldn't deny him anything, especially not after the rough way he'd treated her mouth with his cock.

He hadn't wanted to hurt or scare her, but to teach her how he liked his dick sucked. The best way to do that, he'd decided, was to show her firsthand and let her get used to him immediately. No reason to pansy along and then suddenly change the rules later. He'd have it done right the first time.

She'd balked at his first thrust, fighting her ability to breathe, and he thought he'd lose her, but he'd talked her out of her anxiety and everything after had been copasetic. She'd sucked him like a pro and damned near taken the head of his cock off in the process. He liked seeing her mouth so tight around him he'd actually popped out of her.

Cole shed the rest of his clothes and strode naked into the bedroom where Bri had stretched out on the bed like a perfect submissive. He liked that thought. Her breasts, nipples still taut, had flattened somewhat with her supine position. Her labia were shiny with her juices and he could smell her desire across the room.

His cock stirred, rising to half-staff in anticipation, wanting to rid her tight channel of its virginity. He grinned.

Tomorrow when she woke, Bri would find herself bound to this bed, her arms and legs stretched to each post, her abdomen firmly strapped down. She would have almost no room for movement. He would shave her pussy then, while he toyed with her and introduced her to a few new things in her life. One of them would be her bodyguard, Tyler Cannon. And he did mean bodyguard in every sense of the word.

Tyler would lounge on the bed in the morning and watch as Bri squirmed in sheer embarrassment. This would be after he made love to her pussy with his mouth. Something Bri would be helpless to stop.

Cole's cock stood at attention now with thoughts of watching Tyler and Bri together. He knew she would embrace the three of them when she got used to the idea, the same way she'd already taken to obeying Cole's wants.

Tyler tended to be a little more gruff in his demands, balancing nicely with Cole who was more soft-spoken. Both of them affected the same reaction in their women—*if you don't do what I ask, you will be punished.*

Cole opted not to tie Bri up right now. He crawled onto the bed and settled himself between her thighs, his shoulders pushing them wider to make more room.

"Grab the headboard, Bri, and do not let go or I will flip you onto your stomach and spank you. Then I'll tie you up, fuck you with my tongue until you're on the verge of an orgasm, and leave you."

She shivered, her breasts jiggling with the force, and her stomach muscles tightened. Her slender fingers grabbed on to the spindles above her and squeezed until her knuckles went white.

Cole lowered his head and chuckled against her pussy, causing Bri to arch her back and squeak. God, he loved her. The thought flooded his brain, just another piece falling into place like a puzzle where everything seemed right with Bri.

He blew on her and she gasped, waiting for his first touch. Very delicately he licked her, starting in the tight hole of her cunt and working his way up between her pretty, pink folds and stopping at her clit. He pressed the tip of his tongue against the nub and held it there. She squirmed beneath him and he let her, knowing without tying her down, he'd never keep her wildcat body still.

This was her first time being devoured by a man's mouth. He would let her feel everything, let her move on his tongue, give her what she wanted before he took her completely.

He swirled his tongue around and around, in and out of her tight sheath, lapping up her cream, inhaling her scent, until she was writhing beneath him. Poor baby, she was the loudest creature he'd ever fucked. Her cries would be heard throughout the house, and his entire staff would know exactly what they were doing.

He mentally shrugged. She panted and moaned and squealed as his tongue danced around her pussy, propelling her higher and higher.

Cole separated her folds with his finger and circled her hole, spreading her moisture on his finger. Then he pressed into her tight core, catching her hips as they shot off the bed with her ear-piercing scream. She arched so high his finger nearly slipped out of her.

After he settled her body again, he went to work, alternately licking her in long and short strokes. He penetrated her sheath with first one then two fingers, tickling her G-spot in rhythm with his tongue on her clit. She never once let go of the headboard. In just a few minutes, he'd worked her into a frenzy.

"Please, God. Please, Cole, please!" She screamed into the arm where she'd buried her head, her body writhing as if in extreme pain.

He would have liked to get some nipple play in, but with one set of fingers shoved inside her and the other working hard across her hips to keep her steady, Cole had no choice. He would have to wait until later to work more on those sweet berries.

Cole lifted his mouth from her honey and drove his fingers in as far they could, stretching her virgin's barrier and preparing her for his cock.

"God, don't stop, don't..." Her head shot back and forth on the pillow as she pleaded with him to end her misery.

He laid into her once more with his mouth, sucking her clit between his lips and biting gently.

She screamed to wake the dead. Her pulse beat ferociously as her orgasm ripped through her body, and her vaginal muscles clenched around his fingers.

He climbed higher on the bed and knelt between her thighs, keeping one finger on her clit to keep the sensations rolling. Her eyes were squeezed shut and sweat beaded on her forehead. She never opened her eyes as he reached for a pillow and propped her hips up with it.

Still caressing her clit, he brought the broad head of his penis to her wet channel and pushed gently against it, watching it disappear inside her body. Her eyes exploded open on the new invasion and she squirmed against him, moaning loudly, begging for more.

Cole pulled out, his cock bobbing up and down, slick with Bri's dew, weeping with his own. He'd never taken a woman skin to skin, but he wasn't about to stop, no matter the consequences. This was for him, not her father.

"Don't stop...you...can't," she cried.

"No, baby, I won't stop." He pressed forward again, lodging his cock's head more firmly inside her this time.

Bri bit down on her lip and shifted against the sudden pain of his cock stretching her tight pussy. He pulled back a tiny bit, watching the relief cross her closed-up face, then thrust deeper.

Her hips jerked, impaling herself on his cock, and she screamed with the pain Cole could see quickly become pleasure. He resisted the urge to pound into her wet warmth for the space of about three seconds, and then his cock took over.

He lifted her knees into the crooks of his elbows, placed his palms on the bed beside her shoulders and drove into Bri's sweet nectar. Her vagina pulled at his erection, sucking at it like her tiny mouth had done earlier. Their bodies slapped together where they were joined, his balls connecting with her rosy butt hole with each thrust.

He reached a hand between them and separated the skin hiding her rejuvenated clit, exposing it to his pelvis. She grunted below him with the force of his penetration.

Bri screamed, indicating her orgasm. Cole groaned and buried his cock as far as it would go, her climax triggering his own. His semen shot deep into her womb, an experience he'd never felt. Just the thought that his boys could, even now as he collapsed on top of Bri, be swimming to meet her developing egg, made his cock twitch.

Their sweaty bodies stuck together as they lay heaving in a pile on the bed. His penis was still embedded in her body, a place he would be content staying in. Only the wheezy breath emanating from Bri's lungs made Cole move.

He pulled from her body, careful not to hurt her anymore, and felt deprived of her body's heat. He rolled to the side and off the bed. In the bathroom he found her discarded jeans and the inhaler in her pocket. Back at her side, he held it to her lips as she lay nearly asleep, still wheezing.

"Come on, Bri." He wiped a sweaty lock of hair from her face. "Breathe for me, baby." She did, though not deeply enough for his liking.

Damn it! He'd intended on waiting to take her until his doctor had seen her, and now he'd caused this. He pressed the medicine down again, delivering another dose, and this time Bri took in a bigger lungful. She coughed as the medicine worked its magic.

Bri reached a small hand out to him and grasped his wrist. Her eyes opened sleepily and she smiled.

"Thanks." Her lids drooped and a second later she was sleeping, her breathing less noisy.

Jesus. She was so fragile. He and Tyler would have to be gentle with her until they got this asthma under control. He was afraid if they went too far with her, she would have an attack behind a gag and not be able to tell them. It was possible both of them would be so enthralled with what they were doing, they wouldn't notice she was having trouble.

His other problem was she was as responsive as a rocket. He wanted to suspend her in pleasured agony with tons of play and they wouldn't be able to do that if she shot off each time they touched her. He would have to devise some kind of attack plan to keep her on edge and not over it.

Cole wet a washrag with warm water and set about cleaning her thighs and between her legs, wiping away the evidence of his ownership. She never stirred and he chuckled. For a woman who hardly spoke, she sure could pack a wallop in the screaming-orgasm department. He covered her body with the sheet he pulled from beneath her, hoping she could get in an hour's nap before the doctor arrived.

*** *** ***

"So, young lady, I want you to get this preventative filled and take one every night. Here are some samples to use until then." The doctor Cole had called handed Brianna a small box of pills he'd brought with him and a prescription for more.

She listened as he explained a new round of treatment for her asthma. The man was very nice and she liked him, despite the fact Cole had been behind his visit.

Why couldn't she just accept Cole's generosity? He'd done more for her today than her father ever had.

"Any serious attacks, you call me or get to the emergency room. I heard quite a bit a wheezing when I listened to your lungs. Your father ought to be shot," he grumbled under his breath.

Brianna curved her lips into a half smile. It was good to know not everyone thought Andrew Wyatt was a god, no matter how hard he played at being one. She wondered what the doctor would say if she told him the reason she was here in the first place was because Andrew thought Cole could get her pregnant with a son. Now, not only did she have one supporter, but two. Both the doctor and Cole seemed more than willing to step up to the plate and go to bat for her. It was an alien feeling.

"And now I will leave you. Get some more rest if you can, you look exhausted."

You would be too, if you'd just had sex for the first time. Oh God. Her face burned with mortification.

Wait. He was leaving? Other than listening to her lungs and asking her a few questions about previous treatments, he hadn't even looked at her yet. She assumed when he'd first come in the room, Cole following close behind, that he'd want to do a full exam.

"I...you're leaving?" Damn. Couldn't she keep her mouth shut? If the good doctor wanted to leave, why was she trying to stop him?

He sat on the bed beside her and patted her knee like she was a child. "Was there something else you wanted?"

"No." She shook her head and smiled to soften her rather harsh rebuttal. "No I just thought—"

He laughed. "You thought Cole wanted something more, didn't you." There was a twinkle in his eye. "He told me you might think I was here to do a complete physical on you. I'm not, rest assured. He called and asked if I would take a look at your asthma, that's it, not to deem you healthy enough to bear children."

She flushed again. Cole had already told him about her circumstances.

"Yes, he told me everything," the doctor said, reading her mind. "Like I said, I personally think your father should be shot, but I know Cole, and I know he'll do the right thing. Trust him, he's a good man." He stood and walked to the door.

Trust the man who was blackmailing her? That was kind of a tall order. Deep inside though, she did. It probably had something to do with the whole support issue again. Somehow she trusted Cole Masters to take care of her and her brother.

Chapter Three

Gentle fingers trapped her ankles and pulled gently, separating her legs and leaving her wide open. Cole knelt between her thighs. He licked his lips like a big cat, anxious to devour the feast before him.

He bent over her, tickling her hardened nipples with his chest hair, and stretched her arms above her head.

"Stay," he whispered, then emphasized the soft command by pressing her wrists into the mattress.

She shivered and her tummy flipped as he described in detail the things he wanted to do to her. His erection bobbed against her mound as he rocked gently above her. The rough hairs of his thighs scratched along the sensitive skin near her apex, and she squirmed under him.

If he would just touch her clit, she'd explode. Between the erotic words and the constant rubbing, her body was primed.

"Wake up, sleepyhead."

Brianna turned to the interruption. The words were a deep baritone, different from the ones Cole still whispered in her ear.

"Let's go, little one, time to get up."

The voice intruded again, sweeping her away from the bliss just seconds away.

Except Cole was gone now, leaving behind a wash of cool air on her heated skin.

Brianna groaned and buried her cheek deeper into her pillow. So soft. Her pillow had never felt so heavenly. When had the maid replaced it? She'd have to remember to thank her. She inhaled, not ready to start another day. Not after the dream she'd been having.

And why exactly was she dreaming about the man frequently found on the cover of a magazine?

Bits and pieces congealed, forcing her to remember where she was and why she was there. The limo, her father demanding she give him an heir, his threats to Scottie, the doctor visit, Cole. How could she possibly forget what had happened between them? She came awake slowly. That's why she'd dreamed about him. Who wouldn't? She smiled, thinking about all the things Cole had made her do and then done to her.

Then reality hit. She was here in absolute carnal bliss while her brother was home and vulnerable to their father's neglect and condescension. She wanted to bury her head in her pillow and make it all go away. The exotic feelings of happy bliss were gone and a guilt-ridden sadness had taken over.

Her body felt like mush and she couldn't get it to obey her command to roll over. The room was still black so it couldn't be morning, but she was wide-awake now. Brianna's nose tickled so she reached for it, only to be brought up short by the fact her arms were tied to the bed, stretched out above her head. Her nose tickled again as her tummy plummeted. The room wasn't dark. She was blindfolded and bound to the bed spread-eagle, and naked, based on the cool air on her flesh.

She had not been dreaming at all, merely incorporating reality with sleep.

She panicked, her heart thudding, her breath gasping as she tried to move, but couldn't wiggle so much as an inch. A feather light touch tickled her left breast, causing her skin to break out in goose bumps.

A deep chuckle sounded to her left and Brianna jerked her head. The laugh had been different from Cole's. It was lower and easier, like it came from someone who laughed a lot. From the same person whose voice had jerked her from the heated dream and all the things Cole was about to do to her.

"I know you're awake, Bri."

"Cole?" She turned her head, searching for the source, knowing it hadn't come from her left.

"Yes, sweetheart?"

There he was, at her feet. She swallowed. "Who's here, Cole?"

"You're right. She does swallow when she's nervous."

Two distinct laughs reverberated in her ears. She fought to see through the blackness, to see who she was dealing with, while her body thrilled and betrayed her. She felt the slick evidence of her desire pooling with the thought of being touched by two men, even when her mind screamed it was wrong to want to be fucked by more than one.

Apparently the rumors about Cole were true. She should feel embarrassed, outraged that they were both looking at her naked body, but she couldn't summon up either emotion.

The feather, at least she thought it was a feather, stroked her exposed neck like a lover's caress, soothing her despite her fears.

"Shh. Relax," the man whispered against her ear.

His fingers, she assumed they were the unknown man's, trailed a blazing path down her throat, along the valley between her breasts, pausing to circle her areolas. His fingernails scraped gently across her abdomen and stopped where he dipped into her belly button. Brianna sucked in a breath at the exquisite feelings. It was then she realized she was also bound to the bed by a strap across her hips, preventing her from even arching her back.

Her face grew red as she smelled her own arousal.

"So soft," he murmured.

"Like silk," Cole agreed.

The strange fingers continued their journey, learning her body and tangling in her pubic hair. Brianna bit her lip, silently begging him not to stop, to touch her clit, to make her come, but he withdrew his hand. She groaned in disappointment and sank into the mattress.

"Let's shave this off. I want only skin here."

Brianna gasped at the gruff command, startled by his abrupt change from gentle to demanding.

"A hot, wet towel, Bri." The bed dipped between her legs where she guessed Cole climbed closer to her.

"Cole, stop. I don't want this. Don't do this!" She sounded pathetic, she knew, but God, they had her tied to a bed and were going to shave her pussy.

"You promised, Bri. It was part of our bargain. You agreed to do anything I asked of you. Now I'm telling you. You will do whatever we tell you. Now, shh. We want you naked, Bri. We want to feel your smooth skin as we lap up your juices. It's just hair, baby."

"We? We?" Brianna squirmed as best she could. "Who is we? Damn it, Cole, at least let me see who we is!"

"My name is Tyler." He said this one second before an intense pain shot through her nipple. She screamed and tried to dislodge whatever was pinching her now distended, hard nipple. The tight bead was soothed as quickly as it had been punished by a wet tongue rasping over it. Immediately the pain became a pleasure sizzling its way to her vagina, drenching the hair which would soon be gone.

Suddenly she didn't care what they did to her pubic hair, she just wanted one of them to touch her.

"A screamer, huh?"

"I told you she was."

"You made it sound like she was a little noisy, not loud enough to shake the rafters."

"Yeah, well, I wanted you to see for yourself."

Brianna mentally pictured Cole's shrug and nearly cleared her throat as they talked about her as if she were not there. Her nipple was throbbing beneath its clip, a delicious, warm tingle, now that the pain had dissipated.

"Please," she begged, her body again doing the speaking for her.

"Please what?" Tyler asked.

There was no emotion in his words, as if he didn't care that he had a tied-up, naked woman laid out like a sacrifice in front of him.

"Please, touch me. Cole," she offered at the last second, remembering his desire for her to say his name.

"You remembered. I'm impressed."

He touched her then, laying the hot washrag over her mound. The heat scorched her raised clit, adding to the searing pleasure/pain at her nipple. Her body hummed with desire.

Warm lips closed around her free nipple, sucking it into a hard peak. Tyler, she thought, rolled it around his wet mouth, consuming her. She moaned and ground her head into the mattress. Cole laid his hand over her washrag-clad pussy and pressed in rhythm with the mouth sucking her breast. Its rough texture antagonized her clit, but did not give her enough.

She wanted to touch someone, to feel the hardness of Cole's body against hers as he devoured her. Even more perverse, she wanted to slide her hands over Tyler's skin, to learn the shape of him through touch, if she would not be allowed to look at him.

His lips released her tight bud with a pop one second before it was clipped the same as its twin. She screamed and bit into her lip, tasting the coppery fluid leaking onto her tongue.

"Oh, God. Oh, God." She thrashed her head back and forth, denying the shooting pulses of pain grinding away at her chest. Her nipples burned deliciously as a tongue once again soothed the offended flesh. One touch to her clit would send her over the edge, but now she realized the rag had been lifted and the hot wetness was gone. A cool breeze wafted through her pubic region, cooling her desire.

"Please!" she pleaded, unashamed now that she was so close.

"Not yet, little one." Tyler chuckled, his words coming from close to her breasts.

"You cannot leave me like this," she cried out in frustration and excitement.

"I can do whatever I want. This is my show today. Cole had his turn yesterday." There was an almost whiny quality to his voice. A picture crept into her head of Cole and Tyler as children, fighting over a toy.

Brianna shivered. Why, she wasn't sure. Picturing these two men as children should have completely erased her desire. Instead it increased it. Cole laughed, leaving Brianna wondering why.

She heard a slap and envisioned them giving a high five. Then she felt a slap, sharp against her clit, and jolted as much as her bindings would allow. Her pussy reheated and renewed its traitorous begging to be touched.

It was rewarded when someone slid two very large fingers inside her vagina. Her muscles, sore from their use last night, protested at the sudden intrusion.

"So fucking tight. How does she taste?"

Cole grunted. "Like heaven."

Tyler's fingers worked in and out of her, stretching her and spreading her juices. She felt it as it dripped down along the skin between her vagina and anus. Brianna licked her lips and bucked her hips unsuccessfully against his hand.

She flinched and yelped as another slap landed against her clit. Tyler's fingers ceased their movement.

"Be still, or I'll pull out of this tight little cunt and leave you to lie here all day."

Please don't do that! Brianna nodded and swallowed.

She felt Tyler separate the folds shielding her clit with his free hand and his fingers resumed thrusting. The palm of his hand rasped against the tight bundle of nerve endings, firing off an explosion deep in her womb.

"You smell so fucking good."

The rasp of a zipper sounded to Brianna's right and had her jerking her head in that direction. She smelled Cole's essence and knew he'd just taken his cock out of his jeans. Her lips itched to kiss it, to lick the small drop of fluid she knew would be present at its tip.

"Come closer," she breathed, her nostrils flaring at the scent so close, yet so far.

Her clit rang out as she was slapped a third time, and she screamed again. The pain quickly flared into pleasure that soared to her nipples.

"Again." Just one more slap and her body would sing.

"No. That's my mouth right now, Cole. Don't get any closer to her."

"Aye, aye, captain."

"And you, little one, you don't give the orders, I do. You'll come when I say, not when you want to."

Brianna groaned. Her orgasm was so close. She squeezed her buttocks in frustration and pulled at the restraints on her wrists.

"Christ," Tyler snarled.

She growled as he yanked his fingers out of her pussy, the fullness suddenly gone. Then two sets of hands were on her wrists, stilling them, and rubbing where whatever was around them had ground into her skin.

"I will not let you hurt yourself," Tyler gritted out. "There are better ways of getting your pleasure through pain."

"Please." Brianna felt the cords in her neck strain as she begged to be sent over the edge of the climax still lingering so close.

"Shh," Tyler soothed as he rubbed his soaked knuckles along her cheek.

She whimpered and cried out. She turned her face into his hand and kissed his roughness.

"Uh-uh. You aren't going to win by crying. Where's the bit?"

"Right here," Cole answered.

There was a rustling above her. She twisted her head following the noise, her heart pounding. What was a bit? It sounded like something you would use for a horse.

"What are you doing?"

"Ensuring that you're quiet."

"What?"

"Relax, Bri. We'll make you feel good," Cole assured her.

* * *

Tyler dragged his tongue across her clamped nipple, stilling her impulsive reaction with his palm on her belly. It quivered beneath his hand letting him know just how turned on she was.

When he'd seen her this morning with her dark blonde hair fanned across Cole's pillow, his cock had thickened painfully beneath the fly of his jeans. Cole had lifted his head and looked over her shoulder at him, then nodded. Without a word spoken, Cole had seen the hunger in Tyler and rolled out of bed. Bri hadn't even twitched.

Within minutes they had conferred in the sitting room and set to work, gathering supplies and binding her to the bed.

"Open your mouth." He wanted her quiet this first time, but didn't know why. The erotic image of her completely restrained filled his mind, hardening his length even further.

Brianna went mutinous below him. And what woman wouldn't? She didn't know him, didn't know what she was getting into. Her lips pinched tight and she shook her head. He knew exactly what would get that little mouth open. He thrust his fingers into her hot sheath again and Brianna gasped, losing control of her mouth. Before she could close her jaw again, he fitted the bit between her teeth.

She fought against the cylinder of rubber, and he chuckled. "Good girl." He jerked his head at Cole. With his fingers deep inside her, working her into a frenzy, he wouldn't be able to secure the bit. "Tie this one for me, would you?"

"My pleasure."

Cole fastened the bit around the back of her neck before Bri could even think about spitting it out. Tyler walked his fingertips over the sensitive tissues of her pussy. Her neck corded as she arched her head into the pillow. Now she was completely focused on the building sensations in her body rather than the bit.

"I can't fucking wait to get a taste of this little cunt."

Tyler made a dramatic show of licking his lips and slurping like he was ready to devour her, and smiled when Brianna whimpered behind the gag. Cole used a small brush to cover her pubic hair with a generous amount of shaving cream, working around Tyler's hand. Both of them were careful not to touch her clit throbbing just beneath its hood.

"Pleath, pleath, touth me!"

Tyler ignored her, and she growled menacingly around her mouthful of rubber.

He twisted his wrist and circled the inside of her vagina. She could growl 'til the sun went down. She wasn't going to come until he gave her permission.

Brianna squealed when he hit a more sensitive spot. He wouldn't last much longer himself.

"Get to it then," Tyler grunted. He pulled his fingers from her core, and Bri cried out in what could only be considered pure frustration.

"Poor baby, we'll get you taken care of soon, I promise."

Cole scraped along the top of her pubic bone, the blade slicing easily through the hair which was just a shade darker than that on top of her head. Brianna panted through her nose, her thighs tensing in reaction.

Tyler felt a second of guilt. She obviously never shaved herself here, and probably would never have given permission for someone else to shave her. She had said no. Then again, she hadn't really protested too hard. He'd duped her with a pair of fingers sliding in and out of her heat.

Brianna squirmed and moaned as Cole worked, denuding the skin between her legs. It seemed as though each tug of the razor sent little shock waves through her system. Her body rippled, and Tyler couldn't resist touching her again.

He slid his forefinger through her slippery folds, spreading her moisture and causing her to pant around the bit. God, she felt so good. Her hands clenched in tight fists, grasping at the air.

"So fucking wet."

"She's always wet," Cole murmured.

"Good."

Tyler brought his slick finger up over her clit, pausing as she jumped beneath him, then continued over the strap holding her hips down, across her belly button, between her breasts, and finally circled one of her clamped nipples. He leaned over, making Cole pause, so he could retrace the path of his wet finger with his tongue, and taste her. The tiny bud pulsed against the tip of his tongue and he inhaled her scent. Spicy and sweet.

"That means she'll be ready for me whenever I want to fuck her."

He lapped and licked around her nipple, coming close, but never actually touching the straining nub. He squeezed her opposite hip and massaged his way up her exquisite flesh to knead the breast begging for his attention.

Brianna gasped sharply when Tyler released the clamp. Her body thrashed and bucked against her restraints as she was seized by an unexpected climax.

"Fuck."

"Fuck." Tyler echoed Cole's hiss as he pulled his lips from her nipple. "I didn't want her to come yet."

Brianna collapsed into the mattress. Her limbs were loose, her head lolled to the side, and her chest heaved with deep breaths. The orgasm had ripped through her, clearly leaving her exhausted and fighting for breath around the bit.

"I nearly cut her," Cole grumbled. "Take the other one off. It's been there long enough. Let her get the next one out of her system before I start again."

Suddenly alive again, Bri shook her head back and forth and grunted through her gag. Apparently she didn't think she could take another one.

"One more, baby. Give it to me."

He released the second clip and she screamed at the ferocity of her second climax, her body shaking violently with the onslaught. Tyler bent and soothed the aching nipple he'd just released. Cole joined him, licking at the other nipple, until she quieted and shivered one last time.

Tyler couldn't wait any longer. "I gotta have her."

* * *

The bed dipped beside her, causing her head to roll to the side. She heaved breath after breath as her body melted into the mattress. A breeze wafted across her sweat-slicked belly, then the other side of her body dipped. If not for the blindfold, Brianna's eyes would have shot open. Tyler had just climbed on top of her!

"I'm taking the bit out, Bri. No sounds, do you understand?"

She nodded weakly. The hair on his legs tickled her sides and his knees pushed against her armpits.

She bit the rubber to hold back a moan forcing its way up when his balls brushed her chest and his hard cock stabbed her chin. She had such a grip on the gag Tyler had to pry it out of her mouth. Somehow it had become a lifeline. Something to bear down on in the midst of the intense pain/pleasure.

"Move your jaw, little one. Work the kinks out so I can fuck your pretty little mouth."

Brianna whimpered, forgetting she wasn't supposed to make noise.

"I will spank you for every noise you make, Bri. You've been warned. That's one."

Her stomach flipped. She was not supposed to be turned on by the image of a stranger spanking her. Her brain told her it was wrong, her body said, *Please God, spank me.*

"Open your mouth wide for me, but do not suck."

His voice was stern and she swallowed, wondering why he didn't want her to suck him.

"I can see the question behind your mask, little one. You'll see for yourself why you don't need to suck in a second. I want to make this last. Any movement of your lips will be added to your noise infractions."

"Cole, I think the butterfly..." His body shifted above her, his cock brushing against her lips, and Brianna couldn't help poking her tongue out to taste him. "God damn it," he shouted.

Brianna nearly jumped out of her skin.

"That's two little girl." His thumb and forefinger grasped her chin and gave it a shake. "Don't move!"

Cole laughed behind them. "I got it right here."

"Open." Tyler jerked on her chin, pulling it down. A heartbeat later the silky head of his cock pressed against her lips. "Hold very still," he breathed.

She did, holding her breath also, not wanting to even twitch beneath him. He groaned as he worked his way into her mouth. Brianna panicked. His cock was larger than life. Tears sprung in her eyes as the mushroom-shaped head pushed past her lips and settled on her tongue. Already, he was far into her mouth and she doubted she could take much more of him.

She gagged as he sank even further, almost to the back of her throat. Tyler buried his hand in the hair at the top of her head, keeping her from arching her neck.

"Oh, fuck, yeah."

"Told ya."

Her lips quivered, stretched to the point of pain, and her tongue curled involuntarily as saliva pooled in her throat, threatening to choke her if his cock didn't first.

Tyler hissed as if in pain. "Be still."

She nearly cried out. As if she was trying to move! Her body was fighting of its own accord. She didn't have control anymore. Did he know what it felt like to have a cock shoved down his throat?

"Now."

Brianna wondered what "now" meant, then bucked like a bronco when her clit began vibrating wildly. She moaned around Tyler's stiff penis.

"Ah, hell. So much for making this last."

Above her, Tyler began thrusting his hips. His thick cock slid in and out of her mouth as her clit thrummed. She whimpered around him, loving the feel of his soft cock head sliding against her. Each time he pulled out, a trail of his salty-sweet pre-come lined her tongue. She ached to suck him, but he was right. His cock was so tight, there'd be no need, and with her lips stretched so far, she wouldn't be able to suck very hard anyway.

Caught up in the feel of his cock, she squealed when he pulled at her hair.

"Be quiet," he gritted out.

His next thrust slammed into her throat and she gagged around his thickness. Tyler paused there, his breath heaving, his sweat dripping on her face. She jumped, lodging his cock even further, and panic set in.

"Ahh. So fucking tight."

Brianna felt like she did when she was having an asthma attack. Her throat and lungs seized up with the lack of oxygen. Then she remembered what Cole had said. "Mind over matter. You can breathe through your nose."

She fought her body's natural response and let her shoulders sag. She loosened her jaw and slowly inhaled through her nose.

"That's it, little one, relax. You can take me."

He began thrusting again, long slow strokes that had her mentally begging for him to move faster, to spill his come in her mouth so she could taste him. The buzzing near her pussy stopped and Brianna groaned and shook her head against Tyler's cock. She didn't want the delicious sensation to end. She tightened her thighs and struggled against her bindings.

"I've got you, Bri."

Cole's voice brought a sense of relief to Brianna. He was still there, hadn't abandoned her when Tyler had started fucking her. He wanted this, she realized. Wanted to share her. Why, she didn't know, but right now she would do anything to please him. A long finger worked its way into her vagina and she pressed her head back, wincing as her hair was pulled by Tyler's tight fist.

"Want more?" Tyler asked.

How could she answer when he'd told her not to move?

"Good girl. Give it to her, Cole. Let her come. I want to feel her mouth on me when she explodes." Tyler was panting now, his exertion obvious. "Christ, hurry up or I'm going to come first."

The vibrations began again, intensified this time, and Brianna tightened her lips on Tyler's cock. Cole pulled his finger from her channel, deflating her hopes of a quick orgasm. The bed shifted by her hips and suddenly she was full again. Jam-packed with Cole's penetration.

One thrust was all it took to throw her over the edge again. She exploded, squeezing Cole's penis with every tiny vaginal muscle she possessed. She milked each of their cocks as they rocked into her. The vibrations wouldn't quit and as soon as her first climax ended, a second one began.

"Oh, yeah, baby," Cole grunted as he pistoned himself between her legs, his pelvis striking the vibrator somehow attached to her clit each time, sending charged lightning bolts through her depleted body.

Above her, Tyler thrust hard one last time and yelled with his release. Hot jets of semen shot into her throat and she swallowed greedily, licking and sucking him to fruition.

Cole gripped her hips and pumped harder. Tyler slowed his movements until he was just barely shifting his cock, and still she sucked, her lips looser now as she adjusted to him.

"Stop," he growled.

She couldn't. She couldn't get enough of him

"Brianna," he hissed in warning.

Her hips shifted and she realized the belt across her belly was gone, the ties around her ankles removed. Cole lifted her butt in the air and draped her legs over his arms. He grunted as he worked in and out of her pussy, once, twice, three times. The fourth was the final. He buried himself deep inside her, touching her womb and setting off yet another climax.

Tyler pulled his cock from her mouth and Brianna shouted. She ground her hips against Cole, wanting to get closer, even though they were already closer than two people could get. His cock jerked inside her, bathing her core with his come.

"Son of a bitch!" Cole shouted.

"My sentiments exactly," Tyler reciprocated, breathless.

As Brianna floated back to earth, her shoulders screamed in protest.

"Untie me. Please, Cole?" she croaked.

"Shit." Tyler scrambled off her chest and Cole withdrew himself, leaving her feeling empty.

Two sets of hands reached for her wrists, releasing them. Her arms were rotated forward and she cried out in pain.

"Jesus, baby, we're sorry."

Chaste kisses were placed up and down her arms. They covered her from armpit to elbow, from shoulder to the top of her breasts. They massaged her as she slid into sleepy bliss. At some point Tyler and Cole joined her, snuggling up to her sides, their sticky, sweaty bodies melding with her own.

"Keep your eyes closed, Bri."

Exhausted, Brianna could do nothing but nod. The blindfold was taken off and the morning light sliced through her eyelids, blinding her as though her eyes were open. She blinked rapidly, adjusting her eyesight, then glanced to her right. Tears threatened to spill as Cole winked and smiled at her. His thumb wiped at her cheek and her heart filled with what she could only describe as love. She'd met the man yesterday and today she loved him. It seemed impossible.

"Bri, I want you to meet Tyler Cannon, your bodyguard."

Brianna's smile slipped. Her bodyguard! Cole had just let a bodyguard make love to her? She swallowed.

"I don't understand."

Tyler's hand came across her body and caressed her breast, toying with her nipple. It beaded into a tight point.

"It's easy, little one," he said. "Wherever you go, I go."

She shivered, despite her anger or confusion or whatever the hell it was.

"But why?" She turned and got her first look at the second man she'd ever sucked off. Cole being the first. Tyler's tawny hair was disheveled, leaving him with a boyish look. His eyes were the color of green grass and his lips were wide and crinkled lightly at the corners, suggesting he laughed a lot. His body enveloped hers as he leaned over and took her free nipple into his mouth, sucking her tenderly. He let her go when she moaned.

"You are by far the squirmiest, loudest woman I have ever fucked."

She gasped, incredulous, and he laughed then swooped in again for another kiss to her nipple.

"And I am going to love spanking the sweet little behind of yours for disobeying me."

There was no amusement in his voice this time and Brianna knew he was really going to spank her. Her tummy quivered just as Cole reached a hand between her thighs and smoothed his palm against her newly smooth mound.

Her neck involuntarily arched with the sensations. "Please tell me what the hell is going on."

** ** **

"Come on, little one, you know exactly why you're here." A niggling suspicion clogged Tyler's throat when she shook her head violently in protest. It was confirmed with a glance at Cole's own shaking head. He closed his eyes and counted to ten.

"Please tell me you weren't forced here to have sex with a stranger." He groaned and collapsed beside her when she swallowed. "Fuuuck." He'd tried not to believe Cole when they'd talked last night. As a security person, it was almost impossible not to see motive behind something like this. Now he was beginning to see for himself Bri was innocent, that she wasn't scheming with her father to extort money from Cole.

"I had no idea what my father was up to until he had me locked in the limo and made this announcement. We were already on our way here." Her hand twisted in the air while the other clutched the sheet tightly against her breasts.

Tyler snorted. As if the sheet would stop him from having her. All she was doing was drawing attention straight to the one place she was trying to cover up. Her beaded nipples poked through the thin cotton, making his mouth water.

"You were right, Cole, the man's an absolute bastard."

"Yep. But," Cole said, yanking the sheet from Bri's grasp and laying a protective hand across her smooth, sweaty belly, "what's done is done."

Tyler laid his hand directly above Cole's, loving the way her stomach muscles twitched under their touch. "Yeah, more than once if I know you."

"Hello? Naked woman here."

Tyler growled. "I see naked woman here." He bent down and licked at the pulse in her neck, smiling when she moaned and angled her head so he'd have better access. The woman was a firecracker in bed.

"Please, you have to listen to me."

Brianna pushed at his head, but it was the tone of her voice that had him looking up.

"You don't understand." Her eyes were wild as she stared at him. "My, my father, he, he thought that, that..."

"Slow down, Bri. We don't need you hyperventilating on top of your asthma." Tyler rubbed her quickly cooling arms in an attempt to calm her, while Cole did his best to reassure her with inane words whispered in her ear. They didn't work.

"But my father, he said the, the contract was with Cole Masters, not Cole and his bodyguard. He'll kill you for messing with his heir."

Tyler nearly laughed when she punctuated "heir" by making quotes in the air with her fingers. She was so cute. Naïve, but sweet and endearing. And Cole was right, he was gonna fall very easily for her. He already had.

"First of all," Cole stated beside them, "I don't give a flying fig what your father has in his contract. A 'father' doesn't give his daughter no say in the matter of who impregnates her, and he doesn't presume to take the kid away when said daughter has the baby, then kick her out the door. Secondly," Tyler yanked his head out the way when Cole flung a hand in his direction, "he's not my bodyguard, he's yours."

Tyler grinned again when Bri's gaze darted back and forth between Cole and himself. She looked like a scared doe, with big, round eyes.

"Why?"

"Hey now, don't sound all grossed out," Tyler said, affronted.

"Do you know how much I'm worth?" Cole asked.

Bri shook her head, then seemed to reconsider and nodded. "More than my father is if the magazines are anything to go by."

Tyler sighed, hating Andrew Wyatt more and more. He'd thrown Bri to a pack of wolves and given her no information about the man she'd be "bred" with. He'd gladly choke Wyatt whenever they met.

"You're right. Cole has more money than your multi-millionaire father could ever dream of having. In a nutshell," Tyler said, "Cole's need for security is far greater than your father's. There is security all around this estate. Some you'll see, others you won't."

"But why you, specifically?"

Tyler sniffed his armpit. "Do I smell or something? Is there some reason you don't want to spend time with me?" He tried to give her his best puppy-dog eyes.

A tiny smile cracked one corner of her sweet mouth, and Tyler's heart skipped a beat.

"Other than I don't know anything about you, no."

"Mmm. You know how much I want to fuck you." He guided one of her hands to his stiffening cock and held fast when she tried to yank away.

"Seriously," he said, allowing her to pull her hand back where she felt safe, "I own the security company. Cole and I have been friends since grade school. Most of my business is run from the estate. I had an office built near the front entrance so I could meet with clients. I don't do much hands-on work anymore, but yes, if you go, I go. We won't take chances with your life. Not when there is a real threat of kidnapping, mugging or whatever, because of Cole's name."

"But I don't have Cole's name. I'm a nobody."

Cole snorted and spoke before Tyler could get his mouth open. "I can change that."

"What does that mean?" Bri's voice and breathing shot up to near-panic stage.

"Don't worry about it right now," Cole assured her and plucked at the nipple closest to him.

Tyler jumped when Bri barked out a laugh. She obviously understood more than they gave her credit for. He'd been just as surprised as she when Cole mentioned marriage, if in an extremely roundabout way. Not that it hadn't crossed his mind. He'd heard something different in Cole's voice when they'd talked on the phone last night, and now he could see the difference in him. Cole wanted Bri like he'd wanted no other woman.

"You're crazy. My father will never let that happen because then he would have no control over my baby."

"Exactly," Tyler and Cole said together.

* * *

Brianna's brain scrambled. What these two gorgeous, naked men were telling her was insane. Almost as bad as her father's scheme to get an heir.

She scrambled out from between their hard, male bodies to stand at the side of the bed.

"Why do all men think they can run roughshod over all us women's lives? I mean, I've been dumped by one arrogant penis into the lap of another one.

"Sorry, *two* arrogant penises," she clarified when Tyler's eyebrows rose. Both men looked down at their growing cocks and Brianna gasped, suddenly aware of her own nudity. Her face heated beyond capacity and she shielded her body with her arms.

"No way!"

Cole catapulted himself to his knees, his semi-erect penis bobbing up and down. "You promised you would never cover yourself in front of me."

Brianna shrieked and a smart-aleck remark leaped from her tongue before she could stop it. "I promised you, Cole, not him," she said with a nod to Tyler.

"Ooh, you are so going to get paddled for that," Cole promised.

Brianna shivered, unsure of whether she was scared or excited by the notion.

"Yeah, well she's got at least four coming from me for all the noise and wiggling she did while she sucked me off," Tyler threw in.

In a flash, both men towered over her, their erect cocks jutting out and stabbing her belly and hip. She felt dwarfed by their size because she was, in fact, very much smaller than they were. Her five-foot six-inch frame had her staring at their throats, which made them what? Somewhere between six and seven feet tall? She gulped down the bubbling hysteria rising in her.

"You or me?" Cole grumbled above her.

"Me, then you." Tyler threaded his fingers through her hair and planted his lips on hers. They were soft and warm and made her forget everything.

"Right." Cole's response jerked her mind out of the gutter and she ripped her mouth off Tyler's.

She laughed. It was either that or go insane. They were both going to tan her hide. Like some recalcitrant child, she was about to be spanked. Not for stealing a cookie from the jar, or breaking some priceless piece of art she'd been told over and over not to touch, but for squealing too much while they fucked her. She was in a surreal world. Didn't men like it when their women made noise in bed?

She held up her hands to ward them off. "Now wait, we're getting way off track here. We were discussing why you think I'm suddenly not going to have my own name anymore."

Brianna yelped as the world turned upside down. One second she was standing upright, the next, she was looking at the floor. Her stomach was pressed against two rough, hairy thighs, her butt was thrust in the air, and her nose nearly hit the floor. It would have too, had she not thrown her hands out to catch herself.

She was mad. Until yesterday, when her father had forced her into Cole's house, Brianna had never been manhandled before. Now she was being turned over a knee for a spanking. It didn't matter that thought sort of thrilled her.

"Stop! Please, can't we talk about this?"

"Oh, we'll talk about it. Later."

Smack!

The first blow landed sharply against her left butt cheek, surprising Brianna with its force, and causing her to bite her lip. If not for the hand between her shoulder blades holding her down, she would have launched herself off Tyler's lap. Her bottom stung with a thousand needles. Tears flooded her eyes with pain and mortification. Even as she squeezed her cheeks together, a rough hand stroked where it had just injured her tender skin.

"God, she's got the most beautiful ass I've ever seen."

A slow burn flooded her pussy, radiating from her affected butt cheek. She squirmed, wanting to feel more.

"Stop moving," Tyler growled.

She stilled a split second before another slap rang out. Tears sprang to her eyes, blurring her vision, and she tasted blood against her lip. Oh God, she would not survive this. These were not gentle taps, they were blows, meant to cause pain. Too bad she couldn't complain. Not when the pain led to her clit humming in pleasure. One touch would send her over the edge. Just one. The hand between her shoulders stroked down her spine, leaving goose bumps in its wake. She arched into the touch.

"I said." *Smack.* "Don't." *Smack.* "Move." *Smack.*

Brianna screamed with each slap, her butt on fire now. She clenched her legs together, hoping for some friction to ease the ache sizzling at the apex of her thighs, as Tyler soothed her aching cheeks with his fingers.

"So pink, so pretty."

She dropped her head so close to the floor she felt her bangs brush the carpet and moaned with the sensations. She was so close to a climax. Her mind reeled at the implication. How could a spanking have brought her to this point?

"Again," she begged wantonly. Tyler chuckled. One hand spread her thighs and rubbed her labia, spreading her juices, but never touching her throbbing clit. She bit his leg, the only thing she could reach with her mouth.

"That's it, bite me, fight it, baby. I don't want you to come yet."

His finger stroked her, trailing up over the skin between her vagina and back hole, and pressed against the tight rosebud. Brianna panicked and jerked her mouth off his leg. She arched away from his thighs and Cole's hand now holding her down again.

"Don't..." Her cry was muffled as she gritted her teeth, while Tyler's finger sank into her anus. The pain was scorching, burning her unused muscles, overwhelming the pain she thought she'd felt with the spanking.

"So fucking tight. We'll have to start small, Cole."

His finger retreated, slipped back into the juice coating her pussy, then returned to her anus, gaining further entry into a space Brianna had never imagined would be penetrated. She fought the intrusion, wiggling her backside, trying to shake him off at the same time trying to get closer, but he and Cole held steadfast.

"Relax, Bri," Cole coaxed. "We need to start stretching you here so you'll be able to take our cocks."

Impossibly, the blood drained from her head where it had pooled from being upside down.

"What do you mean?" she croaked. No way could they fuck her ass. The idea made her shiver.

Cole knelt bedside her and put his lips next to her ear.

"Exactly what I said. We intend to fuck your tight little asshole. It'll feel so good, Bri."

He pushed her hair out of the way and got closer to her.

"Imagine, one of us in your pussy, one of us in your ass. You'll be so full, so tight. The sensation will set you off like an explosion. We'll do it too, often. You won't know where we begin and you end. Let Tyler in, let him stretch you, so your body will accept the plug."

The image of Tyler and Cole both fucking her at the same time had her body relaxing. They were both so good at getting her off, and neither of them had hurt her. Even the spanking, though it had hurt at first, had left her wanting to come. Instinct had her screaming that she could trust them with her body, even despite the fact she knew nothing about either one of them.

Tyler's thick finger retreated and his body twisted, nearly throwing her off his lap. Seconds later something hard touched the sensitive hole of her rear and she felt a cold wetness. She tensed.

"It's just a lubricant, Bri, I don't want to tear you. This will help."

Then his finger was back, working and wiggling its way inside her as her tight muscles eased. The burn remained but had lessened as his finger pushed in and out of her.

His thumb brushed her clit. The sensation in her pussy matched the one in her full ass, sending a shower of sparks throughout her body. She thrust back, trying to grind against Tyler's hand.

"That's it, Bri," Cole whispered. "Let yourself feel. Come for me, baby."

A climax ripped through her body and her clit pulsed wildly under the pad of Tyler's thumb, unrelenting in its demand.

She sagged over his legs, sated and exhausted, so boneless her forehead grazed the carpet.

"Cole, get your licks in now while I'm buried deep in her ass."

Brianna's eyes popped. They weren't done yet?

"No," she cried, just as Cole's palm landed squarely on her still tingling backside.

"Oh, yeah, that's nice. She's got fantastic muscles back here that'll squeeze a cock to bursting."

Tyler's finger retreated from her back hole slowly.

"Feel that, Bri? Your ass is gripping my finger, trying to keep me inside. It knows what it wants even if you don't."

He patted her butt, sending little shock waves, and she damned every traitorous nerve ending in her body. Tyler stroked her back for long minutes, soothing her tattered body, allowing her time to get her bearings back before helping her to stand. She still wobbled as the blood rushed from her head.

Cole gripped her arms to steady her as he spoke. "Go, get a shower and dress. We'll meet you in the dining room for breakfast and to talk."

She tried to take a step but her legs gave out. Tyler shot an arm around her, wrapping it just under her breasts. Her head flopped back onto his shoulder, while her vagina, anus and butt still thrummed with pleasure.

"Whoa. You gonna be okay? Need some help with your shower?" Tyler's voice was laced with concern.

Brianna wrenched out of his arms and commanded her cooked noodle legs to be uncooked noodles. She could not take another orgasm. Not right now, anyway.

"I think I can handle it." Her voice cracked and she hated the vulnerability it portrayed.

"Good."

He turned her face with his hand on her chin and kissed her. A kiss so raw, yet tender that her eyes watered. They had used her savagely today, but here was Tyler, kissing her like she was the only woman in the world for him.

"Don't make me punish you again," he growled when he released her lips.

She swallowed and nodded against his lowered forehead, although she wasn't certain she wouldn't want to be spanked again. The fact she'd liked, no loved, what they'd done to her, scared her to death.

Shaking, she fled to the privacy of the bathroom. She needed a few minutes of solitude so she could come to terms with what was happening and reason out the motives for Tyler and Cole keeping her.

She should be demanding they take her home this second. Her mind said this, but her body demanded more of their attention.

Chapter Four

Cole glanced up from the svelte, blonde woman clinging to his arm, to catch Bri looking around nervously. She'd paused halfway down the foyer steps when she'd seen him trying to pry Caroline Grace's fingers off his biceps. At least, he hoped that's the way Brianna saw it.

A slice of her tummy was exposed, peeking out from between the white tank top and loose, mid-thigh, blue skirt he'd chosen for her to wear today. Unless she'd snooped through the other rooms, which he didn't think she'd had time to do, she wasn't wearing any panties or bra. He hadn't left any for her to wear.

He and Tyler wanted her ready to take them at any time, and underwear would just get in the way. His nostrils flared and his cock hardened. She was theirs. He liked the way that sounded.

Watching Tyler take Bri's mouth had made him so hard, he'd had to take himself in his own hand a few times. She'd accepted Tyler as easily as she had him. But there had been another emotion clinging to his subconscious this morning. Something he couldn't quite discern. It was just on the tip of his tongue, a foreign feeling he rarely encountered.

Cole mentally shook it off. There was plenty of time to straighten things out.

Caroline's blood-red, expensively manicured nails walking a path up his arm jerked him out of his musings. Her fingers ended at his shoulder before she swept her palm across his chest and flattened her hand over his sternum.

"Cole," Caroline whined.

"Caroline, it's time for you to go." He wrapped a hand around her wrist and extracted her claws from him.

"Oh, poo, Cole."

She pouted, but acquiesced when she saw the fierce look he was giving her. He turned and scuttled her toward the door.

"What time Friday, Coley?"

God, he'd never realized how shallow and meaningless Caroline was. Maybe that's why he never got past sex with her. Why he'd never felt the desire to stay in her bed after it was over.

"The party starts at seven o'clock. You and your date may arrive at seven o'clock."

"My date? Cole, you are so funny."

She turned back toward him, no doubt to pinch his cheek, and he could see the exact moment she spotted Bri on the steps. Her mouth dropped open, then clicked shut.

"Cole," her voice went from teasing blonde to haughty, "I believe one of your maids needs your attention. She's not dressed appropriately for a servant, either, if you ask me."

He glanced at Bri. Her face had bloomed bright red. She seemed paralyzed where she was, unsure of whether to go back up or come down. Cole found himself wishing she hadn't taken a shower, because then Caroline would see what Cole knew Bri to be. A well-fucked woman. He grinned.

"She's not a servant, Caroline."

"What do you mean, Cole?"

The woman really was dense. "Her name is Bri."

"Brie," she said, her nose rising as if she smelled something distasteful. "Isn't that some kind of cheese?"

"It's short for Brianna."

"Oh, well." She shrugged, dismissing Bri, Cole was sure. "Who is she? A cousin or something?"

"No."

Caroline cocked her head and looked thoughtful for a moment before turning on him with a venomous scowl. Her inflamed face topped Bri's embarrassed one. Her hands fisted at the ends of stiff arms and he could hear her teeth grinding.

"That's not possible," she griped.

Cole shoved his hands in his pockets, dropped his chin to his chest, and sighed. He had hoped to avoid this little scenario for Bri's fragile sake.

"Mornin', Caro." Tyler leaned against the doorframe to the dining room, crossing his arms over his chest and his feet at the ankle.

"Shut up, Tyler," Caroline hissed.

Tyler lifted a hand in the air, palm up. "Come down, little one. Don't mind the tiger here. She's all growl, but no bite."

Cole groaned, then jerked his head up. Tyler had all but admitted to having a relationship with the same "little one" Cole had claimed wasn't a "cousin or something". Tyler was as taken by Bri as he was, or he would never have said anything with an audience. He mentally pumped his fist in the air.

"Cole." Caroline stamped her foot, her face incredulous. Not about what Tyler had said, since Cole didn't think she'd even heard him, but because of Bri, who finally let go of the banister and started down the steps.

"Do not tell me you have fucked this, this...whore, after spending the night with me Saturday."

Tyler straightened from the doorway, snarling. Bri stopped dead about three steps up, her hand shooting to her mouth.

Cole went nose to nose with Caroline, gripping her by the arm.

"Don't you *ever* refer to Bri with anything less than civility." He spun her toward the door once more just as Tyler reached Bri. "And don't be crude, it doesn't suit you."

He opened the door and shoved the dumbfounded Caroline out. She looked over her shoulder and screeched before he could get the door shut.

"You will regret this, Cole Masters."

*** *** ***

Stunned, Brianna entered the dining room on Tyler's arm, the sound of a shrieking Caroline echoing in her ears. She'd been tugging self-consciously at a well-hated skirt, not really paying attention to anything other than the fact the two Neanderthal men wanted her to wear the dratted thing, when she'd seen Cole with that woman in his arms.

A shaft of white-hot jealousy had stabbed through her. They obviously had some kind of relationship. Did Cole honestly think she would stand by while he slept with another woman?

She'd been paralyzed, struck by the revelation she didn't want anybody else laying claim to what she considered hers. The words had not been spoken yet, but her body had already made its decision. And worse, Scottie had never figured into the equation, although she knew with certainty Cole would take good care of her brother.

Seconds went by as she tried to grasp the decision she'd come to.

"I'll say a proper good morning to you now, little one." Tyler wrapped his arms around her and squeezed, kissing her gently on the lips.

Brianna was still too shell-shocked to respond. He held her away from him and looked at her long and hard, taking in everything.

"Hey, sweetheart." His fingers slid into her hair, tilting her head up so she had to look at him. "Don't pay attention to anything that bitch says. She's been trying to weasel her way into Cole's life for a long time. She's only after his money." He kissed her forehead.

"But he slept with her," she whispered. If what she'd just said didn't sound like jealousy, then nothing would. She could kick herself for letting Tyler see her emotions.

Tyler snorted. "So?"

"But today, and last night..." *Shut up!*

"Today and last night have nothing to do with Caroline," Cole said from behind her. Brianna whipped around to face him where he stood in the doorway, looking sexier than ever. His hair was still wet from his shower, his feet bare and his white T-shirt was untucked. He looked like he'd dressed in a hurry. Perhaps because that vile woman had shown up at the door.

"How can you say that? You slept with one woman on Saturday night, then with me on Sunday night." God, she was starting to sound like the blonde bimbo who'd just left. She straightened and held her chin high. "I'm sorry."

"Sorry about what?"

"It's none of my business who you sleep with."

He was on her in two strides. "Let me tell you something." He grabbed her chin, forcing her to look at his face. "First of all, I didn't do any sleeping with Caroline. We shared a fuck, then I left. It was a mutual release of sexual tension."

Brianna couldn't hold back the snort and Cole shook her head, refocusing her attention. Tyler chuckled behind them.

"Secondly, on Saturday I had already dismissed your father's contract as total bullshit. I am not a stud service, and it hadn't occurred to me he would really go through with this. Plus, I didn't know for you there would be some sort of motivation to get you to go along with his idiocy. It wasn't until I saw you the first time that I changed my mind. So you see, Saturday was just like any other day for me, sex and all."

"But...she—she sounded rather intimate with you out there."

Cole shook his head. "She and I scratch each other's itches when need be. I have never led her on or promised her more than a quick roll on the bed."

He lowered his head and kissed her very thoroughly. His tongue plundered her mouth, stroking and twisting with hers until she could do nothing else but wrap her arms around his neck and hang on for dear life. When he pulled away, her mind was even mushier than before. He reached out and grabbed both her hands, untangling them.

"And third, it *is* your business who I sleep with. To ease your anxiety, I would cut off my arm before I would cheat on you."

Brianna sucked in a sharp breath. She darted a glance at Tyler who smiled around the spoonful of choco-puffs he'd just shoveled in his mouth.

"Don't look at me, I don't cheat either."

She squirmed under their scrutiny and tugged on the god-awful skirt again. Cole could have at least left some panties for her. But no, she suspected they wanted full access to her body at all times. Which she would give, damn her traitorous body.

"Stop pulling at your skirt." Cole laced his fingers through hers and led her to a place setting between Tyler's and his.

"I hate skirts," she grumbled.

Both men raised a brow.

"Tomboy?" they said together.

Her face heated, giving her away. "Yeah, so?"

They both laughed out loud. "Imagine. Cole Masters tooling around public with a non-society, nail-biting, no-skirt-wearing tomboy. The press will have a field day with this one."

Cole harrumphed. "Let them think what they want. I don't give a shit."

Brianna sat in the chair and let Cole scoot her in. He leaned over her shoulder, brushed her hair out of the way, and licked her earlobe.

"When you're sitting, keep your legs spread for us," he whispered.

Brianna's stomach plummeted and her pussy flooded with her juices. If it was possible, her cheeks grew even hotter. She slowly hooked her ankles around the legs of the chair so her knees were on the front corners.

Tyler sat on her left, munching the yucky-looking chocolate cereal. Cole seated himself on her other side. His plate was overflowing with fluffy scrambled eggs, bacon, hash browns and toast. He was also having coffee and orange juice. Her mouth watered. She hadn't eaten for what seemed like days.

"What would you like, baby? Eggs? Bacon? Or that gross stuff Ty's shoving down his throat?"

* * *

"Hey, there is nothing wrong with my choice of cereal." Tyler picked up the box and flicked the side of it. "See, it says, 'part of a complete breakfast'. The only thing that would make this breakfast more complete would be if I sat Bri on my plate, spread her legs and ate her."

He threw his head back and laughed at the horrified expression on Bri's face.

"Mmm. She does sound good," Cole murmured. "But what would go even better would be for her to suck us off while we ate."

Bri's face flushed wildly. Tyler took another bite of cereal while Cole leaned in to nibble on her ear. "We'll start those lessons tomorrow," Cole whispered. She audibly swallowed.

"For now, here are the rules," Tyler said, causing her to swing her head in his direction.

"Rules?"

"Absolutely."

"I'm a grown woman, I don't think I need rules."

Tyler snorted. Reality was about to knock her for a loop.

"Like I said, the rules." He paused while Cole fed her a forkful of eggs. "You don't walk out the doors without one of us with you." Tyler watched her jaw as she chewed, and his cock hardened remembering the sight of her mouth wrapped around his hard length. He cleared his throat. *Get through the basics first, moron.*

"Reporters will do anything for a story, including camping out around the corner, waiting for someone to leave the estate."

"But no one escorted that woman out."

Cole chuckled but Tyler snorted again, then they spoke at the same time.

"*That* woman doesn't rate an escort," Tyler growled.

"Caroline can take care of herself," Cole said with a shrug.

Bri's gaze moved back to Cole.

"Are you saying I can't take care of myself?"

His eyebrows raised. "I'm saying, I don't want you to have to."

"No, you're protecting your investment."

"I haven't made an investment, Bri. Your father offered me money for my sperm. At the time of conception, I was supposed to relinquish all rights to *my* child," he ground out. "I don't see that as an investment."

She looked shocked.

"Furthermore, I never signed the contract and I won't ever sign it. But you are ours, Bri. Don't even try to refute that."

Tyler wrapped his fingers around the nape of her neck as Cole's open palm caressed her erect nipple through the fabric of her tank top. She shivered against their hands.

Tyler leaned closer. "There's something about you neither Cole nor I can deny." He nuzzled her throat, laving her with his tongue. "We've decided to keep you."

He smiled when her head lolled into him and she whimpered. He laid his free hand on her knee and slowly dragged it up the smooth skin of her thigh, bunching up her skirt at the same time. Her legs shook as Cole added his hand to her other leg.

They reached her apex at the same time.

"Feel good, baby?"

"Mmm." She sucked her bottom lip in.

Simultaneously, Tyler and Cole rubbed at the bundle of nerve endings hidden in her folds. Her knees spread even further of their own accord and her head fell back on the arm Tyler had stretched along the top of her chair. Her hair tumbled down, tickling at his elbow.

With his teeth Cole raised her tank top, exposing the nipple closest to him, and proceeded to nibble and suckle her.

They worked their middle fingers along her soaking slit, spreading her cream, and played at her entrance. Bri's panting and crying got heavier and louder.

Tyler looked at Cole and nodded. They pressed into her together, stretching her tight sheath. Her tiny muscles gripped them as they finger-fucked her. Her nipples, a dusky brown, stood at attention, one being sucked relentlessly, the other still hidden beneath her tank.

"I...please...I..."

"What, Bri, what do you need?"

"To come," she shouted.

"Then come," Tyler whispered.

She exploded around their fingers, arching her back in the chair, her butt slipping off the edge. Only his and Cole's fingers still inside her kept her from falling on the floor.

Bri collapsed as her body descended from its plateau and they pulled out of her.

"I don't even know who I am anymore."

"Don't worry, little one, we know who you are." Tyler kissed her sweet lips, offering her his tongue. She pulled at it, no longer shy about what she wanted.

Cole smoothed her clothing back in place then leaned over his place setting to eat like he had not just been responsible for shattering the poor girl between them. Tyler smiled. He knew exactly how Bri made both of them feel.

"Damn." He turned to his bowl. "Now my cereal is soggy." He reached for a new bowl and the milk, grinning at the stunned, dazed look on Bri's face.

"So, cereal or eggs?"

"How can you act like nothing is going on? What about my brother? Cole promised—"

"Relax, little one. Scott is, as we speak, being packed up and readied for the trip over here." Tyler massaged her shoulders and squeezed out the tenseness seizing her muscles. Her breath was starting to wheeze again in her agitation and that was the last thing he wanted to happen this morning.

"How...how did you get my father to let him out of the house?"

"With a little taste of his own medicine. I'm serious," Tyler said when Brianna looked wearily at him. "As soon as Cole told me how your dear old daddy had gotten you here, and the conditions you'd given us, it was a no-brainer. I called him up and told him, as the head of security, of course, that Cole would not touch you until your brother had been sent over to the estate."

"Don't even begin to tell me he just said, 'sure, no problem.' My father has hidden Scottie from the world since the day he was born. No way would he let him out if there were even the slightest chance someone would find out about him. And this," she waved her arms in the air, "has a much more than slight chance of blowing up in my father's face."

"Yes, but I think the old man is greedy enough about getting his perfect heir that he doesn't care about what happens to the son he already has. And I told him Cole would never attempt to touch you while you were so agitated about your brother. He laughed when I said that by the way."

"I'll bet he did," Cole interrupted.

"No bet needed," Bri murmured.

"But then, when I mentioned a rape would sully Cole's image, and thereby his own when Cole announced to the public why he was raping the daughter of a fellow businessman, he sobered right up and let me know he would pack Scott's bags immediately."

Bri bit her delectable bottom lip, which made Tyler's cock stir to life again. A perpetual state for the last twelve or so hours, it seemed.

"I have a room being prepared for him and have requested a tutor," Cole stated as he forked up another heap of eggs and brought them to Bri's mouth.

"Oh he's...mmph." Her lips closed indignantly around the fork, cutting her off.

"You, of course, will have the final say in any of the decisions made regarding him," Cole continued.

"Cole. Tyler."

Tyler's heart skipped. He loved hearing her say his name. She looked so sad for some reason, as though what she was about to say would hurt them or something. He ached to make her world as easy for her as possible.

"The thing is, Scottie, he's got a few—"

Tyler reached out and grasped her hand. "We know. He's blind and deaf."

"Partially deaf, and most of the time he can hear just fine," she clarified. "It's just, I spend a lot of time with him. I'm like his anchor, the one stable thing in his life. I can't see how this is going to work."

"How what's going to work?" Cole blurted out. "You're here, he'll be here, we'll be here. For both of you."

"Cole's right. We'll get anything you need for Scott. He'll have a hell of a better life here than at home. At least here he won't be shut away in some back corner of the house, unseen, unheard."

Bri's face burned red and he knew he'd hit the mark. She was embarrassed by the way her brother had been hidden away from society and that she'd been unable to do anything about it.

"But I get the feeling you guys are going to monopolize all my time with your..." she gulped and turned even more red, "...needs."

"Needs?" both he and Cole stated together.

"Yes," she hissed. "I'm not wearing any underwear, does that clue you in?"

"Absolutely." Tyler laughed and Cole's hand slipped under her skirt again.

Tyler held up his hand and fingers in the universal Boy Scout signal. "I promise to set aside free time from my *needs* everyday so you have time with your brother."

"Me too."

Bri growled. "Neither one of you has ever been a Boy Scout, I can tell."

Tyler leaned in and kissed her. "It'll work out, I swear. Now eat, you're too skinny."

Chapter Five

"He's here, Cole, my brother's here." Bri was just a tad bit more than giddy, Cole thought as he watched her practically jump up and down near the front door. Tyler was helping the young man get out of the car, a hand on his elbow.

The morning had been long and restless for Bri, who was waiting on proverbial pins and needles for Scott to arrive. No amount of cajoling or sexual innuendoes had persuaded her out of her eagerness to see him.

"Hmm. He looks normal to me. Ouch." He winced as her hand smacked against his shoulder.

"What did you think he would look like, The Elephant Man?"

He laughed as one corner of her mouth curled in contempt.

"No, baby, I just didn't know what to expect."

"Be nice to him, or so help me God..." she snarled.

"Or so help you what?" he asked, arching his brow.

She paused, looking at him. "I won't...suckyouoff."

Cole cupped his ear and pressed his lips together, trying to hold back the smile. "What was that? I didn't hear you."

"You heard me, you swine."

"Did you just call me a pig?" He threw his hand over his heart and put on a seriously wounded face. "That hurts, after all I've given you."

Her lashes flew upward as did her hand to cover her open mouth. For a second he thought she was scared she'd said something bad, but then he saw her eyes crinkle. The little shit was playing with him. And here he'd felt bad for hurting her feelings.

"Hi, honey we're home." Tyler pushed on the door and jockeyed with Scott to get through the opening.

Bri squealed, causing all three men to cover their ears and wince. "Scott!" She launched herself at the teenager, scaring both Tyler and Cole into action, thinking she would knock the kid over, hurting both him and her.

They hadn't needed to move at all because in a split second, Scott spread his feet, bracing himself, and threw his arms wide, catching his catapulting sister in mid-air. Somehow, amazingly, he had known what she would do, and reacted.

Cole and Tyler stared at the pair as they squeezed the life out of each other. An outsider would see a couple who'd been long ago separated. It irked Cole that he felt a spurt of jealousy over the fact she loved her brother so much, when he wanted to feel her tiny little body wrapped around his in the same manner.

Scott was a big guy for his age, and probably wasn't done growing yet. He stood about five foot eleven, and had muscles that shouted a lot of time spent in the gym. Cole supposed if he'd been kept locked up his entire life, he'd probably turn to working out also. Something to fight away the injustice. In a few years, it wouldn't matter if Andrew Wyatt kept him hidden away. The boy would be able to take him out with one punch, then walk out of his prison and never look back.

"I'll get the bags out of the car," Tyler said once he could see there was no danger of falling or dropping by either party.

"God, I've missed you," Bri said, and Cole heard the quiver in her voice.

Scott laughed and squeezed her one more time, then dropped her feet to the floor and made sure she was standing before letting her go. Cole's estimation of the kid shot through the roof. He knew how to treat a lady, even if he'd never been around them.

"You've only been gone a day and a half, squirt." His gaze landed somewhere over the top of Bri's head, unable to focus on anything but the black space that had been with him since the day he was born.

"I know, but that's longer than ever before. What did he say to you, Scottie?"

Scott's shoulders slumped. "Do you really want to know?"

Cole stood at attention. The jovial mood was about to turn ugly. He wanted to put his fist through the wall. Fuck Wyatt and his contract, the bastard. The man would get his comeuppance one way or another for treating his kids the way he had. Cole would see to that.

"Yes, I want to know."

Scott sighed, looking resigned, like he knew his sister wouldn't give up without knowing exactly what her father had told him.

"He said, and I quote, 'That bitch sister of yours has somehow gotten her lover to want you. Pack your bag, someone's coming to get you.' Then he went on to rant about not telling anyone who I was, etc., etc."

"I'm sorry, Scottie."

"Don't be, I can handle him."

Scott turned and seemed to look right in Cole's eyes, making him itch to straighten and flick the piece of imaginary lint off his shirt. How had the kid even known he was here? He had yet to make a sound.

"Tyler told me about what's going on here, sir, and if you're the lover my father referred to..."

Shit, what had Tyler said to him? Cole cleared his throat. "My name is Cole." His voice sounded lame even to his own ears.

"If you hurt my sister, I'll kill you."

"I would kill myself before I hurt your sister, Scott."

Scott's empty stare told Cole he was thinking, and then the kid nodded and said, "All right then."

Tyler walked in just in time to hear the threat. He, Cole, and Bri breathed a collective sigh. How Wyatt thought his son wouldn't measure up was beyond Cole. The kid had more gumption than three-quarters of the men in the world. He wouldn't have to prove himself to *Cole*, that's for sure.

Scott swung around and faced Tyler. "You feel the same way?"

"I do."

"Good, cause I really didn't feel like killin' anybody today. Too messy." He grinned like a Cheshire cat.

"You are a shit, you know that?" Bri laughed and grabbed her brother's elbow, guiding him across the foyer to the staircase, where she proceeded to tell him how many steps were in front of him. Bri stopped about halfway up and looked over her shoulder, twin tracks of tears glistening on her cheeks.

When she mouthed "thank you" to him and Tyler, Cole's heart stopped. He knew then he wanted to marry her. And for Tyler to do the same, illegal or not. It didn't even matter they'd only known her for less than two days.

* * *

Tyler stood rigid, the indebted look on Bri's face paralyzing him. "What the hell just happened here?"

Cole chuckled. "I'm not sure, but I think the kid just threatened us with death if we hurt his sister."

"Yeah, I got that part. What I don't get is how he knew where we were. He looked at least in my direction, if not directly into my eyes." A shiver ran the length of his body, leaving goose bumps in its wake. "I think the kid's got a serious sixth sense."

When Tyler had arrived at Wyatt's house, he'd introduced himself to the young man who'd answered the door, thinking he was just another servant to the ungrateful Andrew Wyatt. "I'm Tyler Cannon, Mr. Masters' security specialist, here to pick up Scott Wyatt."

Now Ty laughed as he thought back to the way he must have looked standing there speechless, in front of Bri's brother, who was obviously much more capable of getting around than Bri had led them to believe.

"I know who you are," Scott had answered. A butler had joined them at the doorway and handed Scott's bags to Tyler before turning to Scott and discreetly reminding him there were three stairsteps about four paces forward. Scott had lifted his chin and marched out the door, confident as he took the steps, then waited, his left elbow sticking out slightly, for Tyler to guide him to the limo.

It had been downright freaky in the limo on the way over here. They'd held an almost adult conversation, when Tyler had been prepared to act like a babysitter to a frail, simpering boy who couldn't see or hear.

Hmm. He could think of some delicious ways to punish Bri for allowing him to think the things he had about her brother. There was nothing weak about the kid. Obviously in his relatively short, parentless life, Bri had nurtured him into a strong, determined man. One who didn't care if he was blind and couldn't hear well.

Tyler had a lot of respect for the kid. Respect that made him hate Andrew Wyatt all the more. How could the man not see what his son had become? How could he be so callous, to dump Scott like a leper just because he couldn't see? Scott had overcome his disability, why couldn't his father?

"That sixth sense might just get us in trouble here. I don't think we'll be able to hide anything from him, that's for sure."

Tyler's attention snapped back to the present and he shrugged. "I already told him why he was coming here. He knows his sister was blackmailed with the threat that his father would throw him in an institution if she didn't go along with his scheme. I'm pretty sure he also knows Bri traded her body for his safety."

Cole winced beside him. "Ouch. What'd he say?"

"Well, let's see, he laughed when I told him about the institution and claimed Bri always felt threatened when his dad mentioned sending him away. Then he told me very sternly he knew his sister wouldn't whore herself, not even to save her baby brother. So he figured that there must have been something about Cole Masters she liked, and if she was happy then he wouldn't stand in her way, no matter what his father claimed he could do to him."

"Intuitive, ain't he?"

"That's not all. About halfway over here, he says, 'you want her too, don't you?'"

"Damn." Cole chewed on his lip like he was contemplating how to atone for their sins. "What did you tell him?"

"The truth. That both you and I were interested in his sister."

"And?" Cole twisted his hand in the air.

Ty shrugged again. "He got really quiet. Then he said if when he got here, he sensed that his sister was scared or unhappy, he would make our lives miserable."

Cole laughed. "Why the hell is Bri so worried about him? Sounds to me like he can hold his own."

"My sentiments exactly. I've got to get over to the office for a while. There was trouble last night with one of my operative's cases." Tyler swung toward the door.

"Yeah, go, go. I'll give them some time alone, and we'll meet you here for dinner."

"'Bout six?"

"Yeah."

Tyler skipped down the front steps, digging for the keys in his pocket, and smiled. He and Cole had been thrown for a loop today. At least they wouldn't have to walk on eggshells around Scott. He was sure the kid could hold his own with both of them, and give back double what they dished out. Not having a male role model sure hadn't hurt him much, Bri had seen to that.

Tyler's heart skipped a beat and his cock hardened beneath his jeans. She was theirs, and he couldn't think of a better woman to fill the position. Damn, he wanted her again, wanted to feel the tenderness and compassion she felt for Scott, wrapped around his hips as he pumped into her heat.

It was going to be a long day.

* * *

"You look good, squirt."

Brianna looked at her baby brother who had somehow, in the very recent past, become a man. She wondered how she'd missed it, then smiled. "Oh yeah? And just how would you know what I look like?"

"I can feel it in you. You're happy. Are Tyler and Cole the reasons why?"

Damn, she never could put anything past him. She wouldn't be able to lie to him either. He had an uncanny knack for knowing when she was. She stopped in the hallway, not wanting to disrupt his step counting. Not even a nuclear bomb could do that, but still.

"I don't know, Scottie. I've only known them for a day and a half, but already I feel more...relaxed."

"Sex'll do that to you, I guess."

Brianna lifted her hand to smack him on the back of his head but he intuitively turned and blocked it with his shoulder. "And just what do you know about sex?" she huffed.

"Nothing, in person." He shrugged and a big grin split his face. "But it sounds like fun in the books."

"I see that I'm going to have to start censoring your listening material, young man," she teased. "And furthermore, this is not a conversation I want to be having with my brother."

"Yeah, well, maybe I'll talk to Tyler, he seems pretty cool. I bet he knows a lot about the female species..."

More than I'm willing to share with you. Brianna slapped her hands over her ears. "La, la, la. I can't hear you."

Scott laughed and started walking again, without the benefit of his sister's guidance.

"I ought to let you find your room on your own, you rat."

He grinned again. "Won't be the first shin bruise I've gotten because you made me do it on my own," he said over his shoulder.

"You're about to get another one. There's a table, one o'clock about three..."

She wasn't quick enough. The table wobbled precariously on two legs when Scott stepped into it. The vase sitting on it pitched forward and fell to the carpeted floor with a thud, breaking into several big pieces.

"Oh shit, I'm sorry, Brianna." Scott knelt down and felt for the broken pottery.

"Stop it, Scottie," she hissed. "You'll cut yourself. I'll get it."

"I'm sorry, I didn't mean to—"

"Scott." Brianna grabbed his arm and turned him toward her, angry that one little incident could change him from the confident young man he'd come in as, to the frightened little boy he'd been years ago when their father was around.

"Everybody okay?" Cole strode down the hall, anxiousness bracketing his mouth.

"Yes..." Brianna said quickly.

"I'm sorry, Mr. Masters, I'll pay for the..." Scottie looked down at the ground, "...whatever it was. I swear, I just knocked into it on accident."

Brianna wanted to scratch her father's eyes out for making his son this way. Her throat knotted and her stomach turned, watching him grovel to Cole for a vase that had gotten broken by accident. If Cole so much as said one mean thing she would walk out the door, deal or no deal.

Cole looked perplexed. "Are you the same kid who just threatened to kill me if I treated your sister badly?"

Scottie gulped and wiped his palms on the thighs of his jeans. "Yes, sir."

"Cole." There was a smile forming on one corner of his mouth and Brianna let out the breath she hadn't been aware she was holding.

Scott shook his head and swallowed again. "What?"

"My name is Cole. You wanna call somebody sir, talk to my dad. Did you know you and your sister both swallow a lot when you're nervous?"

He knelt down with them and Brianna couldn't help but be indignant. "Would you stop talking about me swallowing?"

Cole shrugged. "I can't help it, it's one of your many endearing qualities. And it allows me to read you like an open book. Back to the matter at hand."

Brianna and Cole glanced at Scottie who was looking for all the world like he was about to be thrown in the dungeon. His face had drained of color, and his hands fisted tight.

"I could smack you for that open book comment."

"Maybe later, baby. I promise you, Scott, there is nothing in this house you could hurt. My mother had two boys growing up in this house and she didn't leave anything valuable lying around. When my parents moved into a different house, I didn't change anything. So, feel free to run into whatever you'd like. I'd say do your worst, but that sounds like hell on the shins." Cole winked at Brianna.

"You are such a liar," she mouthed back at him, but was glad to see Scottie's hands loosen and the color return to his cheeks. A tear slipped out of the corner of her eye and Cole reached up and wiped it off with the pad of his thumb.

"I'll still pay for it." Scott was as stubborn as they came and Brianna laughed at the mutinous look on his face.

"No you won't. Your room is about five or six...or maybe seven or eight, God I don't know, come on." Cole stood and helped Scottie to his feet then led him to a room directly across from Cole's.

His face red with telltale embarrassment, Scottie closed the door before either she or Cole could say anything further. He didn't even let Brianna give him a basic arrangement of the room. Cole took her hand in his and pulled her into their room.

"The vase was real, wasn't it?" she said as soon as he shut the door.

"Mmmhmm, a Ming, but he didn't need to know that."

She swallowed. "Jesus, Cole. I can't afford to replace a Ming vase!"

"Who's asking you to replace it?" He turned and pushed her until her back pressed against the door, then peeled her skirt up. He teased her clit with his fingers and skimmed through the slippery folds. Brianna gasped into his mouth as he sealed their lips together. The velvet softness of his tongue mated with hers and she sighed, melting into his chest. She wanted him. It took a moment to realize the moaning she heard was coming from her own throat.

* * *
** ** **

"Wrap your legs around my waist," he ground out. He couldn't get enough of her sweet taste. Her moist little mouth was always shiny with something, maybe cherry lip-gloss. Who cared? He'd gladly suck anything off her plump pink lips, as long as there was contact of some kind.

Cole lifted her with his hands on the back of her thighs until she was seated right where he wanted her, her pussy against his rock-hard cock. Only his jeans separated them and the smell of her arousal hit him like a two-by-four. He trailed his hands down her long legs, feeling the silkiness of her skin, before grasping her ankles and tucking them in the small of his back. He angled his hips, supporting her as he reached between them to unbutton his fly.

Bri seemed incapable of anything at the moment, including holding herself up by the simple means of clasping her ankles together. Her mouth devoured his, her tongue lapping at every crevice it could reach, her teeth nibbling, and the sounds. God damn, the sounds. The moaning was tearing him apart, squeezing both his cock and his heart in the tiny vise of her fist. Her complete capitulation undid him.

She wanted him in the most elemental way possible. Tyler too. This kind of reaction had nothing to do with paying off a debt of gratitude for helping her brother. It was her surrender to him, her body's response to him as a man. She wanted him, plain and simple. He would not let her go.

The last button popped out and his erection sprang free. Holding onto the steel rod, he felt between her labia, separated them from shielding her opening, spread her creaminess, and prepared her for his entry. It would be swift and hard. He couldn't wait any longer to be inside her.

Her hands gripped at him, one knotted in the short hair at the back of his head, the other dug beneath the collar of his shirt, scratching at his shoulder.

"That's it, baby, scratch me. How much do you want me?"

"Put it in me, now, Cole, please," she begged.

"Put what in you, Bri?" He fingered her, pressing into her wet heat to his first knuckle. She bowed against him, her back arching and pushing them away from the wall. "What do you want? Say the words, baby."

Her eyes were wild, glazed over in lust, her nostrils flaring with each panted breath. "Your cock, in me, now."

He couldn't hold back the growl as he looked at her face and heard her words. He took his cock in hand and slapped at her clit with the broad, purpled crown. Her head whipped back, thudding against the wall before rolling side to side. Bri closed her eyes and a smile teased the corners of her now puffy, well-kissed mouth. Her panting became grunting, and she bit her bottom lip.

"More," she hissed.

He did it again, looking down between their bodies, shifting her skirt out of the way so he could see where they touched, see the effect he had on her as he played with her. He tilted his hips back, chuckling as she shot hers forward, chasing him, trying to capture his cock. Her groan was pure frustration and her eyes flew open in indignation.

"Shh, relax, I've got you, baby. Just let me get it in you." Cole eased her back and teased her again, penetrating her with two fingers. Her vaginal walls gripped him tightly as he pumped in and out of her. With the pad of his thumb, he covered her clit, swirling around and around the tiny nubbin.

"I'm gonna come," she cried, grinding into his fingers and the head of his cock.

He pulled out of her and she sagged against him, sobbing. Her forehead was sweaty on his neck.

"Please," she whispered.

The plea broke him. He adjusted the engorged head of his penis to her entry and thrust forward, seating himself to the hilt inside of her heaven. Bri's body bucked and her slick walls vibrated around his hardness. Cole waited for her to adjust then grasped her hips and pulled her back down on him. He craved the need to be deeper in her than it was humanly possible to be.

The sensation drove him overboard. He couldn't wait any longer. Cole set up a quick rhythm of thrusts. Her pussy sucked at him, slurping along his length, gripping him. She plastered herself to him and clawed at his back, tearing at his shirt. Her breasts were flattened against his chest, the tightly beaded nipples stabbed at him through the cloth of both their shirts.

"Come for me, Bri."

"Aaahh." She screamed and Cole clamped a hand over her mouth, muffling her as he hammered into her sheath. The contractions of her climax milked him. Seconds later, he felt the fire building in him. His balls tightened impossibly, his penis contracted like the cocking of a gun, and he drove into her, sealing them together until there wasn't a millimeter of space separating them.

His breath heaved in and out of his lungs as the orgasm lit him up, from the tips of his toes to the top of his head. Hot spurts of his release spilled into her body.

Cole rested his drenched forehead against hers, willing his breath back to normal. Bri was breathing hard too, wheezing slightly with each breath. The whistling brought him back to attention. Damn. He had to get her asthma under control. One of these times he wouldn't be able to stop himself while planted inside her, and she'd be in real trouble.

"Slow down, baby. In through your nose, out through your mouth." He tugged at her skirt, searching the pockets for the inhaler she always carried. "Bri, look at me."

Her liquid eyes rose from beneath her lashes. Her mouth parted as she breathed heavier than a normal person should despite what he'd just put her through. He held his own breath as he searched her face for any trace of pain. What he found instead made his heart soar.

She smiled.

Chapter Six

Brianna slumped back in the lounge chair. She could hardly believe it was Wednesday already. This morning when she'd gotten out of the shower, there'd been a pure white, skimpy bikini lying on the bed. The items were surprising since a bikini could constitute a form of underwear, which she'd yet to wear in the three days she'd been here.

The sunlight gleamed off the turquoise waters of the most majestic, tropical, in-ground swimming pool she'd ever seen. All around the pool were huge potted palm trees and foliage that made her feel like she was deep in the jungle. Sunlight streamed strategically through the plantings. It had become her favorite place to get a moment of peace and quiet.

Her skin, slicked with sweat, tingled from the sun's rays and the two sets of eyes peering at her from the window above.

Today, after the guys' usual round of unquenchable, morning sex, she'd donned the bikini they'd chosen for her, grabbed a romance, and headed out for some privacy.

Well, semi-privacy. Their eyes were always watching her.

She shivered, despite the heat. It felt right, being here with them. Scottie had been safely ensconced in the estate and was quickly adapting to his new surroundings. Tyler and Cole allowed him free reign in exploring the grounds and she'd even seen them escorting him wherever he wanted to go.

Tears pooled in her eyes when she thought of the three of them together. Scottie was soaking up the attention of her guys like a sponge. It was the first time he'd ever had male contact besides his pediatrician and a few employees of their father. She'd done the best she could with him, but clearly, he needed some consistent XY influence.

She wished their current circumstances would last forever. It was hard to imagine making Scottie, or herself for that matter, leave when the duty had been fulfilled, because somewhere during the last three days, she had fallen in love with both Cole and Tyler.

The door opened behind her, scattering her thoughts, and she sighed. So much for peace.

"Miss Brianna," Freddy announced, startling her into covering herself as best she could with her arms. Being "less than clothed" with Cole or Tyler was getting easier, *because I always am,* but Freddy was an entirely different matter. The elderly butler was almost like a grandfather to her and had taken an instant liking to her brother. Just last night she'd found them playing chess together. Something she hadn't known Scottie could do.

"This just arrived for you," he said. He seemed oblivious to the fact she was wearing next to nothing, even if it was a bikini, and for that she could kiss him.

Freddy was holding a plain, white envelope with her name on the front.

"Master Tyler said it was okay for you to open it."

Oh he did, did he? Her lip curled, and she thought she saw a smile tug at Freddy's mouth. She didn't need anyone screening her calls or her mail. Jeez. A bodyguard outside the house was one thing, this was another.

She sucked it up. "Thank you, Freddy."

The writing didn't look like her father's scribble, not that she thought he would write to ask about her well being when he'd delivered her here to be mated anyway. Since she didn't know many people, and certainly no one who would care she was here, she was clueless as to whom the letter was from.

She shrugged and slid her finger under the sealed flap.

"Damn," she hissed as the paper sliced into skin. She sucked on the thin red line that quickly appeared, then slid the innocuous white paper out and opened it with a flick of her wrist.

There were two lines of thick, black ink on the paper. Brianna gasped as she read the ominous words:

I have something you want, you have something I want.

Meet me at Tonio's at 2:00.

Her hand clinched, crumpling the paper.

Caroline.

It had to be her. Especially after what Brianna had witnessed between Caroline and Cole earlier this week. How had the woman known that Tonio's was the one place Brianna escaped to whenever possible? Tonio made her feel welcome no matter what time of day it was when she arrived, and was ruthless about keeping the media away from his patrons.

Andrew Wyatt would have had a cow if Brianna had drawn any attention to herself, God forbid. Her punishment would have been threats to Scottie's welfare, so she was extremely cautious of not being in the public eye. There weren't many people who would know her face, but they might connect a name and question her father, and that alone would be an embarrassment for him. Besides, she had no desire to see herself in the papers. Apparently Cole felt the same way since he had yet to take her off the estate. Was he as embarrassed by her as her father was? Was she always to be kept a secret?

She mentally shook herself out of her pity party and glanced again at the now severely wrinkled paper in her hand. Brianna hadn't given the woman a second thought since that first morning. She'd been so focused on Cole and Tyler, there hadn't been time to think about anything else. Besides, why would Caroline care? Surely she could see Brianna would never be able to hold Cole's interest for very long. Soon the newness would wear off and Caroline could have him back.

Not to mention the fact Caroline couldn't possibly have a single thing Brianna might want.

She shook her head. *Wayward thoughts will get you nowhere.*

"Hey, baby."

Brianna jumped at Cole's voice. She balled up the letter, attempting to hide it from his view, knowing it was futile. The man had, like, twelve eyes.

"Hi," she said, a little breathless. The sight of his naked torso made her pussy flood. Again.

"Whattya got there?" he asked as he plopped down, facing her, on the lounge next to her.

"Nothing." If he saw what was written, they'd have her living in a plastic bubble. "Just a note from a friend." She dropped the note on the ground behind her, hoping he would forget about it, then tried to smile but didn't quite succeed.

"Uh-huh." He looked disbelieving, but resigned as if he were going to let it go for now. "So you're telling me a 'friend' of yours just dropped off a note asking how things are going."

Okay, so he's not capable of letting it go. Brianna lifted her chin. "Yes, that's what I'm saying," she lied. What's the worst he could do anyway? Spank her? Bring it on. She blushed.

Cole stared at her for long seconds, almost scrutinizing her, before he finally spoke, breaking the tension. "Fine. If that's the way you want this to go, I'll drop the subject. But don't think it won't come up again."

Of course not. After all, you're the blackmailer, you're the one running the show. Me, I'm just along for the ride.

And what a ride it is. No way could she deny the way they made her feel.

"Well, baby," he said, interrupting her thoughts, "you need to go shopping. Want to get out of here for a while?"

"Absolutely!" she squealed, genuinely smiling this time, his words like a mantra from Heaven. Maybe she could sneak away from him at two and meet Caroline after all. She was too intrigued by the prospect of finding out what the woman thought she had not to. "What are we shopping for?"

"Oh, as much as I love seeing you like this," he pulled her out of her seat and between his legs where he proceeded to ravish her belly with small kisses, "you do need clothes. But Tyler will go with you, I've got work to do." His thumbs brushed against her mound before shimmying beneath the elastic of her swimsuit and nestling between her folds.

"You're wet, Bri. I hope you weren't out here pleasuring yourself." His thumbnail scraped lightly along her labia, then up to her clit. She moaned.

"No, I was just thinking about you. And you would know that since you've been watching me since I walked out the door."

"Mmm. Well, okay then."

He lapped at her belly button and grasped her hips with both hands. She missed his touch between her legs and whimpered. His laughter broke through her sensual fog.

"You taste like coconuts."

"Yes. What? Oh, yeah, my sunscreen," she babbled. God, she was turning into a begging slave to her own desires.

"Show me your nipples."

Brianna whipped her head around, looking for anybody who might be outside. Namely her brother. He didn't have to be able to see to know what they were doing.

"He's with his teacher, Bri, let me see your breasts."

Damn. The man could read her like an open book. She sighed, then complied with his wishes by tugging down the cups of her bikini so her breasts spilled out.

"Fucking gorgeous."

His lips never hesitated, just latched on and suckled strongly, shooting a heated path of need straight to her womb.

"How do I get invited to this party?" Tyler growled.

"Just come o-over," Brianna stammered.

He stepped up behind and sandwiched her between them. His stiff cock prodded her backside through his jeans. His hand circled her throat, shifting her hair out of the way so he could kiss her neck. She tilted her head to give him better access.

Tyler made the strangest noise in her ear as his hands wandered over her belly.

"Coconut. Yum."

Cole laughed. "Yeah, coconut has suddenly become my favorite fruit."

"I don't think it's a fruit," Brianna murmured. Cole stopped licking her nipple and moved down her tummy, dodging Tyler's possessive fingers and sweeping just below the elastic of her swimming suit.

"What would you call it?"

"I don't... Oh, God." Her eyes squeezed shut and she dug her fingernails into Cole's shoulders when his thick finger pushed aside the fabric at her crotch and stabbed into her.

"What was that?"

She moaned. This was an insane time to have this meaningless conversation. "A nut." His finger twisted inside her heat, stroking her G-spot and forcing her to stand on her tiptoes. Her head fell back to rest on Tyler's chest. She felt him nod against her head a split second before Cole pulled out of her, leaving her agonizingly empty. Which they seemed to do a lot.

Tyler tugged the bikini bottoms off her hips and patted each leg, silently asking for her to step out of them. Then he abandoned her backside.

She opened her eyes to see Tyler lying on the lounge chair, his back propped up so he wasn't laying completely flat, his legs straight and together. He'd shucked the jeans in record time because she hadn't even heard him move. His cock jutted out from his groin, saluting her.

"Sit on his cock, Bri."

She braced herself with her hands on Tyler's chest and forced her shaky legs to straddle his hips, holding her vagina just over the broad, purpled head of his erection. A shiny drop of pre-come had gathered in the slit and Brianna couldn't help herself. She slid backwards, leaned over and licked the sticky saltiness off. Tyler hissed and bucked his hips upward, making her take most of his cock into her mouth.

A sharp slap stung her butt, and she jerked forward, releasing Tyler and realigning her slit with his swollen dick.

"Don't do that again," they both growled.

Brianna smiled even as they grabbed hold of her hair with their fists, each pulling her toward them. The semi-pain had her nipples hardening into sharp peaks and her pussy flooding. Cole placed his hands on her shoulders and pressed, while Tyler forced her head down with his hands still locked in her hair.

She sighed as he disappeared inside her sheath. She loved their cocks inside her, the feeling of fullness, as they pumped into her. Sometimes it was hard and fast, sometimes slow and long, but always, when they finally gave her permission to come, it was earth shattering.

At last she was seated to the hilt. Tyler's fingers released her hair and latched on to her nipples, pinching and pulling on them, increasing her need.

Cole's hand pressed between her shoulder blades and soon she was pinned against Tyler's chest.

"Get on your knees, Bri, but do not let Tyler slip out of you."

** ** **

Cole let his hand slide down Bri's sweat-slicked spine, leaving the bikini tied in the back, when what he really wanted was to relieve her of the cumbersome material completely. For now, he liked the way her breasts were pulled tight together by the fabric twisted around them. Her nipples stood out, begging for a good suck, as Tyler manipulated them with his fingers.

Cole stroked his fingertips to the small of her back, listening to the mewling sounds coming from her throat. Through punishment, he and Tyler had gotten rid of some of her very loud screaming in the last couple of days. She was still a screamer but they were working on it and both of them could live with what they had now. It was a mixture of humming or purring, like a kitten when content, and the downright squealing like a cat in heat.

That's what Bri was, a kitten with sharp claws and all. And she was theirs to keep forever. He felt like shouting to the world how much he wanted this woman as his wife. First he and Tyler had to convince her of their plan. Cole couldn't explain why it made him feel so damn good.

His index finger trailed over her tailbone then along her butt crack, ending at the tight rosy bud of her anus. He withdrew a tube of ointment from his pocket with his free hand as he pressed into her back hole to his first knuckle.

"Shh," he soothed as her back arched against his hand and she groaned loudly. They'd played with her ass as often as they could in the last two days, preparing her to take them there.

He withdrew his finger, smiling as she squeezed her cheeks together and let out the breath she'd been holding. Over her shoulder he met Tyler's glistening eyes as he watched Cole prepare to fuck her ass. With one hand Tyler held her head to his shoulder so she was unable to move.

"It's time, Bri."

She whimpered, but Cole didn't know if it was in protest or want.

"Relax, little one," Tyler crooned in her ear. "It's time to feel us both as we fuck you together." His palm stroked up and down her back, rubbing at the tense muscles there.

Cole stepped out of his jeans, glad to be free of the confining denim, his cock bobbing against his abdomen. Pre-come oozed from the head of his dick at the sight of her pussy clenching Tyler's cock. He swung a leg over the lounge so he stood directly behind Bri's beautiful ass. The perfect height for him.

"I love your ass, baby." He grabbed each globe with his big hands and kneaded them, watching as her flesh separated and bunched beneath his fingers. The tight ring of muscles circling her back hole contracted and expanded.

"Oh, God," she cried and Tyler yelped as her sharp teeth dug into his chest, leaving a mark.

Cole spread the lubricant over his throbbing dick, wiping at the slit when it released another drop of come. He spread her crack with his finger and thumb, placed the tip of the tube against her anus, and squeezed a good amount of it inside the puckered hole. She squirmed, backing up to cradle his cock between her cheeks and he pressed his length against her. The head of his cock peeked out at him and he groaned.

He pushed Bri forward, just enough to where his tip slid down her crack to position itself on her tightly puckered hole. He rested one hand on her shoulder and with the other he held his cock, guiding it as he began to enter her. Her muscles spasmed around him and he could have come right then.

"So tight. Relax baby, let me get it in and you'll be fine."

"Hurts."

"I know. It will burn 'til you get used to it," Cole answered. "Take a deep breath for me."

As soon as she did, her anus loosened for the briefest second and Cole drove his cock home. Brianna's head shot up despite Tyler's hand in her hair and she screamed against Cole's violation of her ass.

"It's done, Bri, I'm in." He leaned over her and licked along her neck. "Do you feel us both baby, deep inside you?" He soothed her with his tone, let her adjust to the sudden fullness of possessing both their cocks this way.

She gasped for breath beneath him, not the wheezing of an asthma attack, thank God, but just her getting her bearings.

Tyler's hands caressed her front while Cole ran his over her back, adding to the sensations inside her. Cole slid his hand around her waist, easing between her and Tyler's bellies, and fingered her clit. The tiny nub was swollen and ripe, and Bri was so worked up he felt her tremors on his fingertips.

She was on the brink of an orgasm. He wouldn't be able to keep her from having one if she was this close just from them entering her. It wouldn't be right to try either.

Cole pulled out, allowing Tyler to push in.

"I'm gonna come," Bri cried.

"Go ahead, baby. Whenever you want."

They quickly set up a rhythm leaving all three of them gasping for breath. Bri wrapped her arms under Tyler's armpits and grasped his shoulders with her hands, her knuckles turning white.

"You like that, little one? You like when you're full of cock?"

Bri groaned in response to Tyler's questions. No answers were needed. A climax ripped through her vagina, contracting all of the muscles in her lower body, squeezing both his and Tyler's penises. Cole growled and pumped himself harder as her anus milked his cock. He'd never felt this good. Never.

"You close?" Tyler panted, something Cole had never heard him do. He knew Tyler was just as affected by Bri as he was.

"Oh yeah," Cole answered.

Bri was slumped between them, her orgasm having shattered her stamina, as they slammed into her over and over. Her muscles continued to spasm against their cocks, sucking Cole closer to the edge. Two more thrusts and he was a goner.

He buried himself in her ass as Tyler's hips lifted. Now both of them were as far in as they could go. Cole's cock jerked as his sperm shot out.

"Oh God. Cole. Tyler." She collapsed between them as they spent themselves.

The harsh sounds of their breathing were all that could be heard. Cole stood, still embedded in her tight ass, and rubbed his thumb along her spine. Bri didn't even move.

"You still alive, baby?"

"I not shnur," she mumbled against Tyler's chest, her nose smashed into his pec.

Cole laughed and began to ease out of her, making Bri whimper as he did so.

"Shh," he soothed.

"God, little one. You nearly killed us." Tyler's fingers threaded through her hair as he lifted her head to look into her eyes. She shook her head back and forth.

"No...I...no. Wasn't me."

Tyler laughed and patted her butt. His face turned serious. "I think you'll be easy to keep."

Cole inhaled sharply. Damn. The sudden possessive feeling hit him like a freight train. He couldn't imagine not sharing her with Ty but he wanted more. He wanted all of her, including his ring on her finger. In the end, he just hoped to hell Ty was going to be okay with his plan since polygamy was just a tiny bit illegal in the state of Missouri.

"I'm most definitely happy with that decision," Cole said.

"Hello. Once again, the jelly in this sandwich is being left out of the conversation involving her life."

Cole chuckled. "Sorry, babe." He leaned over and kissed the skin below her ear.

"Like I've said before, you can't keep me. I'm a person, not a toy."

"Mmm, you're our toy. Your dear father delivered you to us personally, and I for one, am not about to give you back."

"I second that."

"Ugghh." Bri's feet hit the pavement as she stood, Tyler's wet cock pulling out of her sheath with a sucking noise, telling Cole just how hot she'd been for them.

"What? You want to go back to him?"

"Want? No, never, but there are a lot of things I *want* I don't get, so how is this any different?" Her hands landed on her hips, thrusting the hard nipples of her breasts out.

Unconsciously, Cole's fingers reached for one and Bri blindly slapped it away.

"Hey," he said, pulling back the offended hand.

Tyler sat up on the lounge, his cock softening now because they were talking about something other than sex.

"What kind of things do you want, little one?"

"What?" She swiveled to look at Tyler, her face skewed like she had no idea what he was asking her.

"I said, what things do you want that you don't get?"

"That's not important," she snapped. Cole tried not to smile when her head swung back his direction. He loved getting her flustered. "My father, once again, is not going to let you get away with this."

"You're worried about him again?" Cole asked. He let his head drop, tired of having this conversation. What the hell, he'd throw it out there and see what happened. "Your father wouldn't be able to say anything if we were married."

"But..." she spluttered and her arms drooped to her sides.

She was totally heedless of the fact she was standing before them gloriously naked. He smiled to himself. Her face, seconds before he and Ty fucked her, had been priceless. She'd searched with wild eyes for anybody who might be able to see them. He should have told her he'd already dismissed most of the staff for the day.

Tyler cleared his throat and Cole wondered if he was going to tell him to back off. "I still want to know what things you didn't get."

Nope, Ty was still stuck on what to get her for her birthday, uncaring about the fact they'd been ignoring him.

"Married? What are you talking about? I don't even know you. You haven't even asked." Her hands shot back to her hips, her lips curled in a snarl, and she stomped her foot, making Cole smile.

She was indignant as hell. He guessed he would be too if he were a woman. As for him asking, uh-uh, not gonna happen. He wouldn't lose her on the principle of letting her choose. Besides, her body had already chosen for her, it was her stubborn pride that was giving her fits.

"You have a say. I'll let you pick the dress," Cole granted.

"Ooh, thanks for being so gracious."

"I'm waiting with bated breath to know what you want," Tyler said.

"Don't get smart with me," Cole rumbled.

"Or what," she spat, not paying any attention to Tyler.

Cole resisted the urge to start counting. "I'm gonna turn you over this lounge chair and smack your tight little ass."

"Please?" she pouted. "I love it when you spank me."

"Lord, we've created a monster," he groaned.

"Could you please tell me what it is you want that you've not gotten?" Tyler's voice rose an octave. He and Bri swung their gazes to him.

"Jeez, why do you need to know so bad?" Bri huffed.

"So I can get you something for your birthday," he answered with a goofy smile.

"My birthday isn't for three more months."

"Tell us."

"Fine." She plopped onto the chair, adjusting her bikini top so it covered her again. Cole let her, feeling magnanimous.

* * *

God, they were like a pair of bulldogs. They got their teeth in something and wouldn't let go.

"We're waiting."

"Give me a sec." Brianna dropped her head in her hands and wondered how they had gone from the absolute best sex in the world to discussing her life-long desires. Things were moving way to fast. One minute she was living a sheltered, unwanted life, the next she was being pampered and fucked more times than she could count, and being told she was getting married. Hmm, that would put a real kink in Caroline's back, wouldn't it?

The scary thing was she wanted it too. She'd come to the point she couldn't imagine them not being around. The problem, however, was they'd never talked about it, simply decided it for her. She wanted love and romance, not just sex.

And now her body was in a perpetual state of arousal thanks to them.

She may as well tell them some of her secret yearnings or Tyler would hound her to death.

"A piercing." She felt her cheeks redden as she mumbled against her hands. Would they think she was weird, or behind the times?

"Where?" Cole grunted.

The single word was not entirely negative, more like intrigued. Brianna lifted her head and looked at them. Tyler swallowed, suddenly sitting at attention. She glanced at his lap. Yep, his cock, softening minutes before, was swelling impressively.

She shrugged. "I don't know. My ear?" She pointed to the top where many people pierced the cartilage.

"That's no fun," Tyler complained. "How about your nipples? I'd love to see a delicate chain dangling between your studded nips."

Brianna's eyes widened and she shuddered. "You're crazy." She covered her breasts with her hands. "You'll never get anywhere near my boobs with a needle."

"Damn." Tyler snapped his fingers.

"Your navel," Cole whispered.

He stared intently at her belly. A strange quiver shot through her tummy. No. Not strange, she amended. Not anymore at least. She'd been feeling the same exquisite need for him since she'd arrived at the estate and Cole had saved her from her demented father.

The idea of having a sparkling little stud sitting in the hole of her belly button intrigued her. Maybe one with a dangly part. She'd seen those on a few girls before. She could probably pull it off. Yeah, she liked the image more and more.

She swallowed and glanced up at Cole. His cock had hardened too and was glistening with a small drop of pre-come. The look on his face was classic. Like one of Pavlov's dogs salivating.

"Yeah." She nodded and licked her lips, her eyes trained on his twitching cock as her tongue came out.

"You like that idea?" Cole stepped forward and wound his fingers in her hair. His glorious penis was just a heartbeat away.

She nodded again, her throat closing to any words trying to come forth.

"Me too." He released her and stepped back, breaking the seemingly endless sexual tension.

"Yeah, yeah, yeah. All right, the belly button. What else do you want?" Tyler groused.

Brianna groaned. She'd never get his claws out of her. "A tattoo?" She peered at them through one eye, the other squinted closed. She didn't want to see their disappointed faces.

Tyler leaned forward, his elbows resting on his knees, his tongue practically hanging out of his mouth. "Where?" Now it was his turn to growl.

Again she shrugged. There were lots of places she'd been thinking about. But that's all it had ever been. Thinking. The small of her back, right above her hipbone in the front, her ankle. It didn't really matter, she'd just always wanted one.

"What would you get?" Cole's voice cracked and his cock jerked.

Somehow the smallest things turned her men on. Her heart raced. Could it be after all these years of being suppressed, she was actually going to get some of the things she'd only ever dreamed of?

"I...I don't know. I've always pictured one of those little tree frogs or a lizard or something. A really colorful one, but small," she said, getting into it. Her excitement faded when both men raised their eyebrows and looked at her like she was crazy.

"Why so small? What good would a tattoo be if you can't see it?" Tyler asked.

She did a double take. She thought they didn't like her choice of picture, but they were more concerned about the size.

He waved a hand. "Forget it, we'll talk tattoo later. What else?"

"Jesus, do you ever give up?"

"Not until we know you have everything your heart desires," Tyler answered, batting his eyelashes and making her melt.

Brianna rolled her eyes. "Oh, well in that case, I'll take world peace."

"You a Miss Universe?"

She took a sarcastic glimpse at her body, then back at Tyler. "Do I look like one?"

"Fuck yeah," Cole grunted.

"Okay, so realistic things your heart desires." Tyler laughed.

All right. They wanted realistic? They'd get it. "A motorcycle."

They screeched at the same time.

"No fucking way."

"Absolutely not."

Brianna shrank back against the lounger, their scared anger rolling off them in waves. Who would have known? "Why not? Lots of women ride motorcycles. I always pictured a fluorescent green one with a matching helmet. One of those speed jobbers that goes really fast and makes the rider look cool."

"Christ." Cole sank onto the lounger next to Tyler, his face completely devoid of all color.

"Uh-uh. Not gonna happen." Tyler's face had turned an unappealing shade of green and his lips pressed together.

"Well, that's a sexist attitude."

"Do you know how many people die on bikes everyday?" Cole croaked.

She shrugged. "I'd be careful."

"It's not necessarily *you* we'd worry about. It's all the other fucking idiots who don't know how to drive," Tyler gritted out through his teeth. His face was slowly turning from green to red. A muscle jumped in his jaw.

If he ground his teeth any harder, they'd crack and fall out. Okay, so maybe she should put them at ease. They were way wigged out about the idea of her being on a bike. She could live without one if it upset them too much.

"All right, so no to the motorcycle." She held back the smile when both of her gigantic, muscle-bound men let a whoosh of air out of their lungs.

"Get out of here you little minx," Cole barked.

"What? What did I do?"

"Now." He punctuated the command with a finger stabbed in the direction of the door.

"Fine." She stood, walked around to the opposite side of the lounger, and retrieved her bikini bottoms and the wadded up letter. Her breath caught in her throat when she remembered what it had said. Somehow, for curiosity's sake, she had to get to Tonio's at two o'clock.

"We'll leave as soon as you're ready," Tyler called to her. She didn't look back, just raised a hand and waved in acknowledgement.

* * *

"She hid the letter the second she heard me come through the door." Cole worked his jeans over his failing erection. Jesus, just the thought of her on a motorcycle had his head and his cock draining of blood. "Damn it." He rifled his hands through his hair. "We should have read it before Freddy gave it to her."

"Who do you think it was from?"

"How the hell should I know? We both know her ever-loving father wouldn't write, and you said not many people even knew of her existence."

"Right."

"Fuck. I don't like this."

"Me either."

"Keep a close eye on her out there today."

"Count on it." Tyler planted his hands on his hips. "She's getting to you, isn't she?"

Cole nodded then swiped his hand over his face. "Yes." He emulated his best friend's stance. "I want it all, Ty. My ring on her finger, my last name behind her first. Am I crazy?"

Tyler stared at him for a second and Cole's heart stopped beating. If he told him anything other than what he wanted to hear...

A grin split Ty's face and Cole released the breath he'd been holding. "No I don't think you're nuts. Well, yeah, I do. You always have been." Tyler slapped him on the back. "But no, about Bri, no. I could hear something in your voice the first time you talked about her."

Cole's shoulders sagged as if a weight had just been lifted and Tyler cocked his head at him.

"What's the problem?"

"How would we do this, Ty? Legally she can only marry one of us." He forced the words out, hoping Tyler wouldn't fight him for the right to marry Bri. After all, they each had a vested interest in her.

They'd shared women for many years, but never gotten emotionally involved with any of them. Bri was the first. Now

Cole recognized the alien feeling that had hit him the first morning. He was jealous. Jealous of the fact he would probably never fully own Bri's heart. On the other hand, he couldn't imagine not having Ty in their lives. Or their bed.

"On paper, Cole. Nobody can tell us how to live our lives behind closed doors. And who knows, maybe someday I'll meet a girl I want to marry."

Cole snorted. "I don't see Bri going for a foursome."

"You never know. Besides, I don't have anybody in mind, and if you don't care about sharing your *wife*, then I'm perfectly happy with how we're handling things now."

Tyler bent and grabbed his jeans from where he'd left them in a heap on the ground and marched toward the house, naked. He turned and called back over his shoulder, smiling and laughing, "A carat, Cole, she won't want anything bigger, and I get the left side of the bed."

Cole laughed and straightened the cushion on the lounge chair where they'd just taken complete possession of Bri's tiny body. He'd never see the seat again in the same way. Then he remembered why they'd been out there in the first place.

They'd made a mistake, not intercepting the letter. He could feel it. As soon as he'd announced himself, she'd startled and crumpled the letter before he could get a good look at it. Her telltale swallowing confirmed his suspicions. She was hiding whatever was in that letter from them. Something he was sure she didn't know how to handle herself.

Chapter Seven

Tyler drove his sporty black BMW with as much finesse as he did everything else. His hands caressed the leather steering wheel the same way they touched her body. With a kind of gentle reverence. When he shifted gears, his touch was light, the shift smooth. Completely opposite her own experience in driving a stick. She could tell he babied this car, just like he babied her. She had to admit, it felt good, for once, to have someone care about her.

"I'm starving," Tyler grumbled and rubbed his black-T-shirt-covered belly. The action caused the hem to ride up, allowing a patch of his delectable abs to peek through.

Brianna's mouth watered as she remembered being plastered against his hard, smooth skin just an hour and a half ago. She was turning into an insatiable nympho. And to think, her father had threatened to hold her down while Cole fucked her. She snorted.

It was scary how much she actually liked to be restrained.

"We didn't get to eat lunch." Tyler's stomach spoke for itself with a loud growl.

"Hmm. I wonder why." Brianna picked at a non-existent hangnail on her forefinger and rolled her eyes, then thanked God for the opening she needed. She would simply suggest they go to Tonio's for lunch.

She jumped when his big, callused palm landed on her knee before sliding beneath her skirt. He massaged the delicate flesh near the apex of her legs. Her knees, wide apart per their "rules", offered him all the space he needed. She squirmed in her seat, silently begging him to go higher, but stopped when he chuckled.

"You saying you didn't like what we did?"

Brianna shifted. "My butt hurts."

Tyler barked out in laughter. "God you've changed. We've only had you for what, three, four days? You never would have said something so blunt when I first met you."

Brianna tried to summon up the telltale redness of embarrassment. She really did. When it wasn't forthcoming, she shrugged.

"Yeah, well I've learned to be that way in the last few days. One of Cole's first rules was never to lie. Surely there are better things to get spanked for." She wiggled her eyebrows.

"You are an imp." He squeezed her thigh one more time then began stroking her skin with his thumb. Back and forth, back and forth.

Brianna slid forward in the seat, trying to urge his hand higher again, but he stopped her by simply pulling his hand away. She blew her bangs out of her face and sighed.

"So, where do you want to eat?"

She nibbled on her lip. At least she could attempt to look like she was making up her mind. The hair prickled on the back of her neck and she knew he was watching her. His eyes were squinted and focused on her mouth, looking all the world as though he were the one who wanted to be biting her lips.

"Um, Tonio's."

Tyler snorted. "That was definitive. Don't you women always use that old standby, 'I don't know, where do you want to go'?"

The little shit was mocking her. "Usually, but today I want to go to Tonio's."

"Yeah? Why?"

"Does it matter? You said you wanted to give me whatever I wanted. Within reason of course."

"You're pushin' it, little one."

They drove the rest of the way in silence, something Brianna was grateful for. It gave her time to think about how she would handle her meeting. Time to stop thinking about how Cole and Tyler were seriously starting to affect everything about her.

Ugh. Scottie is your first priority. In order to keep him safe she would keep her end of the bargain and stay with Cole until her father returned. And pray when she had to leave, her heart wasn't ripped to shreds.

She wouldn't even think about the silly proposal. Hadn't that been said in the heat of passion? He couldn't have been thinking straight at the time. Besides, why would a gazillionaire choose her as a wife?

But God, it would be nice, wouldn't it? To be cherished by not one, but two men? To never have to hide her brother again? Her heart thumped just imagining it. Life couldn't really be so kind to her, could it?

She shook her head. First she had to deal with the small detail about whatever it was her letter writer wanted. Brianna couldn't imagine having something *anybody* would be interested in. She didn't have a life outside of Scottie. That wasn't exactly true. Cole and Tyler were here for her. Sort of. At least for the rest of the week. And that was the hard part. Come Monday, Brianna would be gone. The lump returned with a vengeance in her throat. She wanted to lash out at someone or something, hating how she felt so raw inside whenever she thought about leaving them.

"They proposed to you," her inner voice whispered.

"You're awful quiet."

His words made her jerk in her seat. "Sorry, just thinking." Her voice cracked with emotion and Brianna hoped he didn't notice.

"About what?"

She fudged. "About all that's happened this week. I'm glad Scottie's happy. It's been a long time since he's actually laughed when I wasn't around."

"He is happy. He had a blast yesterday when we played blind golf."

She whipped her head to face him. "What?" She hadn't known they'd done anything together.

"Blind golf. I put on a blindfold and we had to putt toward the hole based on where Cole's voice was and his directions."

That did it. She cried. No one had ever done anything like that for Scottie. They were digging a bigger and bigger hole. One she wouldn't be able to pull herself out of come Sunday. If Cole and Tyler liked Scottie it was going to be damn near impossible for her to leave.

"What's wrong?"

Tyler's tender-laced concern brought forth a new gush of tears. She felt the car veer to the right and stop. He wrapped his big, rough hands around her face, then leaned in and kissed her. His lips were soft and apologetic in their touch and, at the moment, she would give anything to remain under his and Cole's safety net. Except Scottie.

She pulled out of Tyler's embrace and wiped at her cheeks, removing the tracks of tears.

"What's this all about, Bri?"

She laughed. It was either that or cry again. "Nothing." She sniffed and shook her head. "It's just...I didn't expect you guys to pay any attention to Scottie. But instead, you're out there, making your world just like his." She raised her eyes to look at him. "Thank you."

"Aw, little one." His hand wrapped around her skull, tangling in her hair as he pulled her toward him and buried her face in his shoulder. She sniffed again but it was too late. Her tears and snot left their mark on his T-shirt. He murmured soothingly in her ear.

After a minute, she lifted away from him. She blew her nose on a tissue that appeared in front of her as if by magic. Tyler sat quietly while she collected herself but his gaze never left her. It made her feel enshrouded with protection.

"Did you win?" she asked him, determined to put on a happy face.

"Hell no, he kicked my ass."

Brianna laughed. Scottie had swindled them. She had been playing putt-putt with him for years. It was one of his favorite activities. Something they could do in the privacy of their backyard.

"Ready to go now? Or would you rather turn around?"

"No," she shouted, then winced. As she suspected, Tyler caught on and gave her a quizzical look.

He put the car in gear. "I can't wait to find out what's eating you, little one."

There was no reason to deny anything since he'd already seen clear through her. She sat back and tried to enjoy the rest of the ride. An impossible feat when her stomach was twisting up in knots over everything that had happened in the last few days.

* * *

Tyler parked the car at the exclusive restaurant, hesitant about going in. There was a reason Bri wanted to go here. She'd been so adamant about not going home even though she was upset. He'd never met a woman who didn't hem and haw and play up the "you decide" game. Maybe he'd just hung around the wrong kind of women until now. The kind who only wanted things that cost a lot of money and made them look better. Bri was in a different class altogether. Hell, she'd cried because he and Cole had played a game with her brother.

Tyler grabbed the SIG Sauer from under his seat as he got out of the car. Tucking it into his waistband at the small of his back, he walked around the hood of the car. He wondered, not for the first time, if Bri's reactions had anything to do with the damn letter. His hand on the door handle, he surveyed the parking lot and street. No one had followed them and he wasn't expecting trouble, but that didn't stop him from making sure.

He wasn't too keen about going into the expensive restaurant in the first place. It was a Mecca for St. Louis's influential people. Even if Bri wasn't recognized, he would be, as Cole Masters's security expert, if not for his own wealthy status.

Tyler opened the door and his heart missed a beat when he looked into Bri's red-rimmed eyes. Who knew that a little scrap of a woman with asthma, and a whole lot of other problems, would be the one to worm her way into his soul? And Cole's. Then she smiled at him.

"Are you sure they'll let you in?"

He cocked an eyebrow. "Why wouldn't they?"

He got a peek of her shaved mound as she swung her legs out of the car. It was all he could do not to lay her across the seat and fuck her. Instead he grasped her elbow and tugged her out of the car.

"I'm positive there's a dress code that doesn't include old jeans, a T-shirt that's been washed ten thousand times, scuffed boots, and...you're probably not wearing any underwear are you?"

He shook his head. "Absolutely not. But then, neither are you." He reached over the seat and grabbed a lightweight leather jacket.

"Believe me, I am not happy about that fact."

Tyler shut the door and locked the car with his remote before they headed across the parking lot. He kept Bri on his left side and guided her with a hand on her lower back. His right hand was loose and ready if he needed to go for the SIG. He was ambidextrous when it came to firing the weapon, but his first inclination would be to go in right-handed.

"You may not be, but I am. Besides, I've got a nice watch."

"Oh, well then," she scoffed. "You think they have a sign in there that says, 'If your watch costs more than our most expensive bottle of wine, then we'll welcome any ratty jeans and T-shirt wearing man, going commando, into our establishment'?"

"Hmm. You have a really convoluted mind, you know that?" He leaned in close to her ear and squeezed her hip as he opened the door. "I promise, they won't turn me away."

The smell of garlic, oregano and tomatoes bombarded him as they opened the second set of doors, and his stomach growled again.

"Hungry?" Bri tossed at him over her shoulder, grinning.

"I told you I was."

The owner, Tonio, stood with his back to them at the hostess desk. Tyler waited for the brawny Italian to turn and recognize him. Tonio knew who had money and how to treat them. The man was certainly not dumb. He wouldn't have cared if Tyler had shown up in a Speedo. It was one of the main reasons he and Cole visited Tonio's on a regular basis. The other was the way Tonio ran his restaurant. Hecklers, photographers and autograph hounds were strictly off-limits.

Tonio turned to them and Tyler released his hold on Bri's hip. As the dominant figure, size wise, over Bri, Tyler was the first to attract the bigger man's attention.

"Tyler." Tonio's voice boomed in the small reception area.

Tyler clasped hands with Tonio, returning the firm handshake.

"I've missed you, *amico mio*," he said in a thick Italian accent. "Where have you been hiding yourself?"

"I've been on assignment."

"And now you return with a new lady." His eyes twinkled as he grinned.

Beside and a little behind him, Bri cleared her throat. She must have taken offense to being called his lady. Well tough, that's what she was. He turned to introduce her to Tonio only to find her face split by a smile that stopped his heart. She was lit with pure joy, not embarrassment.

"Ah, Brianna, *buongiorno*."

Tyler was stunned. How did they know each other? Tonio leaned into Bri, taking each of her hands in his, and kissed both of her cheeks.

"How are things with your *padre*? And your *fratello*, Scottie?"

Tyler growled uncontrollably at their closeness, stopping only when Bri pulled her dainty hands out of Tonio's beefy ones, turned toward him, and patted his chest. He realized, with her calming measure, he was perhaps being a tad ridiculous.

"They're...unusual, to say the least."

Her doe eyes locked with his and Tyler's groin thickened. He'd show her unusual.

"But now, now you are *con amico mio*. Tyler, he is a good man. Things will be good for you. He is not like your *padre*."

She nodded. "I believe that."

Thanks for the vote of confidence. "There's just the two of us, Tonio," Tyler broke in, his voice gruff.

"*Si, si,*" he answered, but then turned back to Bri. "The same table, no?"

Tyler crossed his arms. What happened to deferring to the man? He let his arms drop when he realized Bri hadn't answered yet. Instead, she was scanning the restaurant, as if looking for something. Or someone. Well, it appeared he had his answer. She *had* had an ulterior motive for coming here.

"That would be fine," he answered for her as Tonio waited patiently. Tyler grasped Bri's elbow and gave her a gentle nudge in the direction Tonio was leading them.

"Who are you looking for, Bri?" He was unable to keep the semi-anger out of his voice.

"Huh?" Her head whipped toward him.

"You're suddenly very preoccupied. I want to know by whom."

At least she had the courtesy to look guilty before she answered, "No one."

His grip tightened on her arm. She was lying through her teeth and he was going to punish her for it later.

Tonio led them to the farthest, dimmest corner of the restaurant, and Tyler felt his heart slow. This was her usual table? Because she didn't want to be seen, or because her father had forbidden her to be? He abruptly felt an overwhelming sense of loneliness he could envision Bri living with from the moment of her birth.

He meant to sit with his back to the wall, facing the door, and any possible threats, but while he was musing, Bri had maneuvered her sweet little ass that direction and planted herself there.

"Aren't you going to sit down?" she asked him innocently, as if nothing weird had just happened.

* * *

It was five minutes to two. Caroline would surely be here any time now. Brianna looked at her watch again. Still five to.

"Gotta hot date?"

"What?" Where was she? There, by the door. Could it be her? The only thing she remembered about the woman was her perfect blonde hair, blood-red nails, and a voice that could shatter glass. You'd think that would be enough.

"All right." Tyler's fist slammed down on the table, making the silverware jump and clang loudly. Brianna startled too, causing the water in the glass she held to slosh out on her hand.

"What's wrong?" she asked, more anxious now that he'd scared the piss out of her. She used the cloth napkin to dry her hand.

"What the hell is going on?"

She squirmed in her seat and fudged. "Nothing."

"Bullshit. If it were nothing, you wouldn't be glaring at your watch every five seconds and looking around the room like you're searching for your lover," he snarled.

Brianna snorted. "I already have two 'lovers' and one of them is sitting right in front of me. Trust me, there isn't another one." She gulped down some of the ice water, almost choking on the amount she'd taken in, and used the napkin again to wipe at the water dribbling down her chin. She must look like a total fool. Tyler would probably go home and tell Cole they couldn't take her out in public again.

"*Buogiorno.*" Tonio's voice boomed across the restaurant and Brianna let her eyes follow the sound. It was her.

The woman accepted a kiss on both cheeks from Tonio and cackled at something he said. Obviously the two knew each other, which meant Caroline was a regular here. Not that

Brianna would have ever seen her, or Tyler and Cole for tha matter, because she only visited during the non-busiest hours of the day. Which led her to wonder again, just how Caroline knew Brianna frequented here.

"Do you see? Your attention is wandering all over the place."

Brianna made a conscious effort to face Tyler again.

"This is about that letter, isn't it?"

"What letter?" she said, trying to sound innocent.

"Don't go there, Bri. You know exactly what I'm talking about."

Their waitress arrived, interrupting them, to take their drink orders. Tyler ordered a bottle of beer and Brianna asked for a glass of iced tea with no lemon.

"All right." She slouched down in her chair when the girl walked away. Why should she keep the letter a secret? It didn't say not to tell anyone, although the thought was kind of implied. "I did get a letter, which you already know since you 'allowed' Freddy to give it to me."

"Smart ass. It's my job to protect you at all costs. Obviously, I didn't do my job if you're so agitated by a letter. I should have read it first."

"Tampering with the mail is a federal offense, punishable by prison time."

The waitress returned with their drinks and to take their orders. Neither one of them had even looked at their menus, but Brianna ordered her usual, the lasagna, while Tyler chose a combination chicken parmesan and fettuccine alfredo plate. The girl picked up both the menus and promised to be back shortly with the food.

"Lucky for me, it wasn't in the mail then, huh? What did it say?"

God, Tyler's security background had just become the foreground. Brianna rotated her head in the pretext of popping her neck, and searched the room again. What she found instead was Caroline, shooting daggers from her eyes, directly across the room. Her face was set in a sneer which seemed to hold contempt for both Brianna and Tyler. She shivered. The woman was pure evil.

"Bri," Tyler snapped, literally with his voice and his fingers. "What did the letter say?"

She straightened in her chair and cleared her throat. "'I have something you want, you have something I want. Meet me at Tonio's at two o'clock.'" She swallowed as Tyler gripped his beer bottle to the point she thought it might shatter.

"And you didn't think to inform your bodyguard of this fact?"

She shrugged. "I have a hard time thinking of you in that capacity."

"Well get used to it. When we're out in public, your safety is my first concern."

"And what's your second?" She couldn't resist the taunt.

"That's two, Brianna."

"Two?" she croaked. "What was the first one?"

"I asked you who you were preoccupied with earlier. You lied to me. Who was the letter from?" he demanded.

"I don't know. There was no name on it," she said honestly. Brianna let her eyes shift back to Caroline who was now strangling her napkin on the table. She raised one delicate arm and stabbed one of those bloody fingernails in the direction of the restrooms, then snarled a silent "now".

Brianna lifted her napkin from her lap and laid it on the table.

"Let's go another direction," Tyler continued.

Brianna sighed. A dog with a bone.

"What do you have someone else might want?"

"I have no idea. Really," she said, rising to her feet.

"Where are you going?" He slapped his own napkin down, looking like he was prepared to do battle.

"To the restroom, Tyler. Settle down."

"Fuck settle down. You were threatened, in case you didn't get that message, and told to meet some anonymous jerk-off here."

"You're attracting attention," she muttered.

"I'll walk you."

"No, you won't. You can watch me get safely to the restroom on my own. They're right over there." She pointed just in case he'd never noticed them in all the times he'd been here. Hell, she wasn't even sure men used the facilities in public places, ever, so it might be necessary to point them out after all. "I'll even let you intervene if any *man* attempts to force his way in. I may even let you break his arm, should he try to accost me, but you will not hold my hand while I use the toilet."

"I don't like this, Bri. We should leave right now."

She watched as he scanned the restaurant, taking everything in. She was glad Caroline had gone into the bathrooms first. "You said you were starving."

"That was before I knew you were being stalked," he gritted out.

"Stalked is a bit strong, don't you think? It was one letter, no harsh language, asking me to meet someone here." God, she was getting good at fibbing. "Maybe I have a secret admirer." As soon as she said it, she knew it was the wrong thing to say to a man like Tyler.

"I'll kill him."

She cocked her head. "I think you would. But first, I'm going to the ladies room."

"Fine, but you bet your sweet ass I'm gonna watch that door like a hawk."

She nodded, then turned to face what was probably going to be a very unpleasant meeting. Her stomach flopped as she walked. She'd never been in a physical confrontation with anyone, but she could see things getting ugly with Caroline involved. The woman certainly looked snobby enough to start a catfight.

Maybe she should ask Tyler if she could borrow the gun she'd seen him stuff into his pants. Yep, that'd go over really well. "Hey, Ty, could I borrow your gun? Caroline's nails look pretty sharp today."

At the door labeled, *Bambina*, Brianna paused and inhaled. Her chest was becoming tight, despite the new medication working wonders the last couple of days. Good thing all the stupid skirts had pockets on them or else she'd be carrying her inhaler in her fist. So far, Cole had thought of everything when it came to her asthma.

She straightened her shoulders. If she stood here for more than a split second, old eagle eyes would suspect something and come running.

Behind the first door, she knew, was a small lounge. Another door closed off the facilities. She pushed through the first door to find Caroline draped across one of the divans, her elegant body seductive and perfect. Brianna was revolted by the thought of how much money had been spent making her look the way she did. And how much of it was Cole's?

She slammed the mental door closed on that thought. She had no reason to be jealous of this pitiful woman.

"Why is Tyler here?" the vampire spat.

"Caroline, I presume?" Perhaps the best way to play this out was pure innocence.

Caroline's mouth and nose turned up in what looked like extreme distaste. "You know exactly who I am, you little tramp."

Ooh, the claws were out already.

"Cole is mine, do you hear me? We are getting married, so you need to get your grubby, slutty hands off him."

"Does *he* know you're getting married? Because I was kind of under the impression he might ask me." Brianna couldn't help but bait her.

Caroline planted a hand on one hip. "Cole would never ask a woman like you to be his wife. He needs someone with class."

"Jeez, I could have sworn I bought some the last time I went shopping. I must have forgotten it. Maybe you could share some of yours?"

"You bitch!" Caroline hissed.

The way she was breathing and twitching had Brianna seriously thinking Caroline might attack her. But then she took a deep breath and folded her arms across her chest. She smiled a fake smile, narrowed her eyes, and Brianna suddenly knew whatever it was Caroline "had", the woman clearly thought it would make Brianna lie down and hand Cole over.

"I know where your mother is."

Brianna's knees collapsed. Thankfully there was a divan directly behind her or she would have fallen on her ass. Never, in a million years, would she have guessed those words would come out of Caroline's venomous lips.

"My mother?" she whispered. Brianna had thought the woman long gone. It had been sixteen years since she'd last seen her. Not that she'd really seen much of her those first ten years, but still. Her mother. It was a chance to find out once and for all why the woman who had given birth to her had left her. And Scottie, the son she'd never known.

Provided, of course, Caroline really knew anything about her mother, that she wasn't just spitting out the first thing she thought would interest Brianna. But then, how would Caroline know anything? Brianna didn't even, though as a child she'd begged her father over and over to find Lydia Wyatt. Her requests had fallen on deaf ears. "She's gone, forget her," he'd say, until eventually she'd done just that.

"I can see I've tempted you. Give me Cole, and I'll tell you exactly where you can find your mother."

Brianna couldn't move. Somewhere deep inside her was a little voice screaming to do anything Caroline asked. *Don't give up this opportunity to find out why the woman ditched you and Scottie.* Then another little voice interrupted saying, *You don't need a mother who didn't have the courage to stick around a sick baby.*

Brianna stuck her chin out. The decision was easy.

"You see, Caroline, Cole isn't mine to give." She knew she was playing with fire when the woman's eyes scrunched together. "If he wanted to be with you, then he wouldn't be with me."

There was no reason to mention she'd be gone by the beginning of next week.

"You'll regret this, Brianna Wyatt. You and your invalid of a brother may want to watch your backs." Caroline stomped from the restroom, her warning ringing in Brianna's ears.

Brianna sucked in a breath. Caroline would have to be spying on them to know about her brother. Unless Cole was still talking to her and had told her about them. That didn't seem right though.

Brianna shook her head. She had to get out of here, but first she needed to decompress. Shocked to the core, she entered the bathroom and sat in the seat next to the vanity.

Her mother?

* * *

Tyler scanned the restaurant again, searching for anyone who looked remotely connected to an anonymous letter for a threatening meeting. There were few patrons at this time of day and he quickly dismissed nearly everyone. They were either too old, or didn't fit the bill.

The back of his neck itched.

Enough was enough. How long did it take one woman to go to the bathroom anyway? *Don't answer that.* Tyler stood. Their food had arrived a few minutes ago and he'd managed to choke down a few bites while waiting for her, but damn it, his woman had been threatened. No matter what she said, that's what it was, and his gut twisted in anticipation of something more happening.

There were few patrons in the restaurant at this hour, so what would it hurt to peek in and see if she was okay? He reached his hand out to push on the *Bambina* door when it swung open and a tiny bit of blonde fury swept out.

That bitch. "What the hell are you doing here, Caro?"

"Tyler," she gritted, her nose twitching. "Just having a little chat with Brianna, not that it's any of your business." She slid past him, being careful not to touch any part of him, and headed straight for the exit.

Tyler's stomach plummeted. He hadn't seen her here, which meant he'd been more occupied with other things than watching out for poison. And Caroline was definitely poison. What had she said to Brianna, and where *was* Brianna? He stepped into the small waiting room. The men's room didn't have this area. You went in, did your business, and left. There was another door in front of him and he pushed it open too.

She was sitting on a small chair next to the sinks, looking pale and shaky. "What happened, Bri?" He knelt in front of her still form and scooped her limp hands into his own. They were cold and clammy. "Talk to me, little one." Her face was pale as a ghost. "Come on, you're scaring me, here. Tell me what Caroline said to you."

Her eyes lifted to his. They were empty. "She said she knows where my mother is."

There was no life in her words.

"Your mother? I thought she disappeared."

"Me too." She took a deep breath, closed her eyes, and pulled her hands from his.

He felt the pain she was so obviously trying to hide as she collected herself and it tore at his heart.

Brianna patted her knees with both hands. "So, what's the plan for the rest of the day?"

Oh no you don't. "That's it? I walk in here to find you in a near catatonic state, and now, just like that, you're ready to go shopping?"

"Yes."

She stood, leaving him kneeling and looking up at her. Tyler sighed. There was nothing he'd like better than to get her away from here, especially since his conscience had been niggling at him from the get-go. He should have stuffed her back in the car and driven them somewhere else. "Fine." He stood too. "Let's go." It was probably best he not ream her in the women's restroom of Tonio's anyway. Despite what Tonio had said earlier about Ty being good for Bri, the bigger man was sure to take exception over a punishment the likes of which Tyler sorely wanted to tender to Bri's sweet little ass.

And Tyler was too horny right now to defend himself against the punches Tonio would probably throw.

He ushered her out of the restroom, reaching for his wallet along the way. He settled their bill with Tonio, made apologies for the uneaten food and the quick exit, and promised to return at a later date.

Tyler scanned the parking lot on their way to the car, but sensed the danger had already passed. Bri's hips swayed beneath the flowing skirt, making his cock thicken and his mouth water. Soon, her bottom would be a throbbing red, marked so by his hand. The thought had him swelling further, the buttons of his jeans digging painfully into the ridge of his dick.

At the car, Tyler clasped her from behind and pressed her against the black metal. Her backside snuggled around his cock as he ran his fingers down her slender arms and placed both her hands on the roof of the car.

"Don't move them." He leaned further in, letting her feel how hard he was, laughing as she gasped.

"What are you doing?" she hissed. Her head swiveled frantically, searching for anyone who might see them.

"Disciplining you. You've been a bad girl."

"When?" she demanded.

He slid his hand from hers, along her arm, over her shoulder, down her back, past her hip, to the hem of her skirt. Her body shivered beneath his touch. Good, she was getting turned on.

"You lied to me about why you wanted to come here."

"I—"

He slapped his free hand over her mouth. "Quiet or I'll gag you." He continued his journey down her body, his palm sliding along her outer thigh, then beneath her skirt until he reached the rounded globe of her perfect ass. "No one can see us, or what we're doing. Spread your legs."

She whimpered against his hand, but did as he asked. Tyler pulled his hand off her lips.

"Remember, don't make a sound or you'll attract attention. I won't stop your punishment 'til I'm through, and since I don't want anyone else seeing your sweet behind, I suggest you keep your cries to a minimum," he whispered in her ear. Biting down on the fleshy part of her earlobe, he watched as she sucked her bottom lip into her mouth.

"Are you wet for me, baby?"

She groaned and he laughed. "I think I'll just see for myself." He caressed his fingers down the crease of her buttocks, pausing at her anus, and pressing just enough to make her wince in his arms. Moving on, he slid his forefinger over her definitely flooding entrance, between her swollen lips, and then flicked at the tiny jewel peeking out from its hiding place.

Her head fell back on his shoulder and her breath hitched in her throat, coming out in tiny little gasps.

"Harder." She squirmed against his finger and he broke the contact.

"Who makes the demands?"

"You do," she pouted.

"You do, what, Bri?"

"You do, Tyler."

"That's right. And right now the only thing you're going to get is spanked." A quick glance confirmed they were still secluded. He raised his hand as much as the skirt would allow and slapped it back down on her fleshy skin. She jumped, but remained silent. He brought his hand down again and then again, alternating between cheeks so he didn't hit the same spot twice.

The slaps were sharp but not near to the point they'd been earlier this week when she'd been draped across his lap. Time to get serious. He landed a hard blow, making Bri jump with a squeal. He dipped two fingers into her pussy, pushing them deep into her heat. A garbled grunt erupted from her slender throat, and her head jerked back and forth on his shoulder. Even more so when he criss-crossed his fingers inside her.

She was on the edge, seconds away from exploding around his hand, and he yanked out of her. It wasn't time yet. Her knees buckled and she cried out in need with his departure, but he held fast, squeezing her against the car to keep her upright. "Not yet," he murmured.

He continued the barrage of slaps, most of them landing on the outer edge of her buttocks because of the way they were pinned on the car.

"Please," she moaned, unable to remember they were out in a public parking lot. "Please, let me c—" He shushed her with his hand again as she thrashed against him.

There, that's what he'd been waiting for. Her begging him to finish her off. He stroked her reddened skin, soothing it, and heightening her senses, then slipped back to her tight sheath. He pumped his fingers inside her then pulled almost all the way out before sliding home again. Tyler stifled her scream with his hand. Her vagina pulsed around him as her orgasm ripped through her.

"I think you'll pay for all this noise later, little one," he whispered in her ear.

With a whimper, she sagged between the car and his body when the violent climax ended. Her hair was sticky with sweat and clinging to her face. She trembled when he pulled out of her. He lifted his glistening fingers to his mouth and sucked her juices off, savoring the taste of her. His cock was about to burst, and his only thought was to get her somewhere so she could ease the tension. A good, fast fuck should do the trick.

Tyler reached around Bri to open the door, and stuffed her into the seat, buckling her seat belt for her. She was boneless, and her eyes were closed, but a smile curved her lips. Tyler leaned in, wiped the hair off her forehead and kissed her brow. If he didn't get in her soon...

He slammed the door and jogged around the hood, jammed the keys in the ignition before his door shut, and threw the car into gear. Bri sighed next to him and her legs fell apart. The musty smell of her sex wafted through the interior. A dressing room, that's what he needed.

Chapter Eight

Brianna barely registered that the car had started moving, let alone it had already stopped and Tyler was opening her door. She blinked and tried to focus her fuzzy, sated mind. They were in front of a row of small, quaint shops housing some of St. Louis' most exclusive boutiques.

"Out." The reason behind Tyler's gruff command strained the fly of his jeans.

She half feared a button would give in to the pressure being exerted on it and pop off. Hmm. Then again, it was at the perfect level for tasting. She licked her lips.

"Now, Bri."

Sheesh, what crawled up his shorts? He was normally in a fantastic mood after spanking her, right now he just seemed pissed off. A tiny muscle ticked along his jaw.

He wasn't pissed, he was horny and unsatisfied. *Well.* She glanced around the parking lot. If he could get her off in public, maybe she could...

A low, rumbling sound emanated from his throat. "Don't even think about it." He stepped back, out of her reach.

Phooey. Her butt protested with a stinging ache as she swiveled on the leather seat and pushed herself from the car.

"Cole is gonna meet us here."

That surprised her. "I thought he was working today."

Tyler grunted. "He was until he found out about your little clandestine meeting."

Oops. Her butt was going to be so sore she wouldn't be able to sit tonight.

"Inside, now." He grabbed her elbow and literally yanked her toward the boutique with a glamorous-looking mannequin in the window. She guessed this is where they'd be purchasing a dress.

"Geez, Ty. Slow down. I hardly think Caroline's going to attack us at a dress shop."

Tyler stopped so fast Brianna knocked into him. Just as quickly he turned and steadied her with his hands on her shoulders. His eyes took in their surroundings.

She couldn't resist whispering, "Is she out there?"

"Wouldn't care if she was." He met her eyes, hunger clawing its way out of his own, and she swallowed. "In case you hadn't noticed, which I know you have, my cock's about to explode. I'd prefer to be inside you before that happens. Now let's go." He took another quick look around before he set off toward the shop one more time.

Brianna balked, pulling at the hand holding her wrist. "You've got to be kidding, Ty." No way was she going to be fucked in the dress shop.

"Look. You owe me. For this whole damn day, I figure. We'll go in a dressing room. It'll take me like two strokes, believe me. Besides," he winked at her, "you need the practice on being quiet."

"I can't do this." Her heart hammered, and she wasn't positive it was entirely due to fear. Her belly clenched with excitement, not that she'd ever tell this Neanderthal, but still.

He leaned close. "You can, and you will."

He tugged again and pulled her through the door. They were promptly greeted by a smiling, bubbly blonde who was more than eager to start collecting the size and style of dresses Tyler all but spat at her.

Could she do this? Have sex in a tiny room where anything and everything could be heard? Where shoppers and clerks would be just a few feet away?

Before she could even formulate an answer to her questions, Brianna and Tyler were ensconced in a nice-sized fitting room, surrounded by mirrors on three sides. The sales person had gathered several dresses en route and hung them on hooks just inside the door. Tyler was quick to let the woman know they wouldn't need further assistance.

Looking a bit miffed but knowing money when she saw it, she left, closing the door behind her. Brianna imagined the woman smiling to herself as she walked away, and assuming Brianna was Tyler's mistress. She guessed she was, in a way.

"Take off your clothes." Tyler's hands flew to his waist and tore at the button-fly.

"Shh." Her face flamed with heat, even as she went to work pulling off her shirt and bra, and wiggling the skirt down her hips. Before she could look up, he was on her.

His tongue invaded her mouth, swirling with her own as his hands cupped her butt cheeks and lifted her. She hoped she was still wet from her previous climax because it didn't look like she was going to get any foreplay.

He staggered forward until her back was against the mirror. Having pinned her, he was able to shift her body weight. He pulled her legs around his waist and she clasped her ankles at the small of his back. They were both breathing heavy as they devoured each other. She clutched at his neck, eager to get good purchase and not weigh him down. The position reminded her of Monday when Cole had taken her in the same way.

Tyler's penis prodded at her entrance, the same as his tongue in her mouth. With one thrust, he impaled himself to the hilt. Her scream was captured by his lips.

She couldn't think. He commanded her mouth and her pussy, drawing everything out of her. He pounded into her so hard her now sweaty butt squeaked against the mirror.

"Is everything all right in there?"

Tyler tipped his head. "We're fine," he growled, his hips never ceasing their rhythm.

The wave built and she didn't want it to. With his mouth gone, she bit her lip to keep from crying out. Her lower back and butt sucked at the glass like a suction cup being pulled off repeatedly. She rolled her head against their reflections, trying to think of anything that would keep her from coming.

Tyler must have sensed something in her because he reached a hand between their bodies and separated the folds of her pussy, exposing her clitoris to the rolling motion of his pelvis.

"No. No, no, no. Please."

Tyler panted and resumed his furious pace. "Yes, Bri."

"I can't. Don't make me." Everyone would know exactly what they were doing in here, if they didn't already. "I'm too loud. Please." She hated being reduced to begging for something she didn't want when she already begged them so much for what she did. She would plead mercilessly for an orgasm, but not here. Not in a public shop when she was so loud to begin with.

He was relentless. In and out he pressed with deliberate intention.

"I'll catch you, I promise." He shifted, bringing her lower so only her shoulders touched the mirror. The angle brought his cock in direct line with her G-spot, which he stroked with ruthlessness.

She grunted in time with his thrusts.

"Come for me, baby."

Bastard. She exploded around him, her hands fisted in his hair as she squeezed him in a tight bear hug, trying to stifle the sensations shooting through her entire body. The metallic taste of blood flooded her mouth when she bit her tongue to keep quiet.

"That's it, baby. That's what I like. Your sweet little pussy milking my cock."

Brianna was done. Exhausted to the point her head fell forward into the crook of his neck. Each of his continued thrusts made her clit tremble.

"My turn," he growled in her ear. She felt him stiffen as he pushed deep inside her, then the hot jets of his release. A climax through which he never made a sound.

They were both breathing hard, their sweaty foreheads plastered together.

"You happy now?"

He smacked her on the butt, and slowly pulled out of her. Her vaginal walls gripped him with a mind of their own, wanting to keep him inside.

"Yes, imp. I'm happy." He dropped her feet to the floor, then steadied her with his hands on her hips before reaching down to pull up his jeans.

She hadn't even noticed he'd only lowered them as far as was necessary. Hell, he hadn't even taken off his jacket. Typical man. From his back pocket he produced a handkerchief. Gently, he wiped his sticky come from between her legs. He swiped at his softening penis, which he then tucked behind the button-fly of his jeans.

Brianna couldn't move, despite the chills taking over her slick body.

"I love you." He dropped a kiss on each corner of her mouth and slapped her hip.

She stared at him. Had he really said that? Just this morning she'd been feeling the same emotion, but she would never have guessed either Tyler or Cole would ever say those words to her. Her heart skipped a beat, and her lungs froze.

"Now, start with this dress, it's my favorite."

Brianna shook her head. Maybe he didn't realize what he said. Otherwise, how could he drop a bomb like that, then tell her which dress to wear?

The dress he'd chosen was a simple, white, flowing slip of silk with spaghetti straps. A hint of lace peeked out from beneath the hemline that would fall to somewhere right above her knees. It was beautiful, elegant and designer.

"How could it be your favorite? You didn't even look because you were too busy trying to jump me."

He shrugged. "I saw it as we walked by and tapped the woman."

Brianna had not seen that. She'd been too preoccupied with what was about to happen in the fitting room.

Tyler stepped out, clicking the door shut behind him and leaving her alone. She sagged against the mirror. Opposite her, another mirror mocked her naked body that had left its mark on the glass. How could she possibly marry these two men? She'd never be able to walk for their constant need of sex.

Plus, she still didn't know what to do about Caroline. The vampire-like woman had threatened Brianna with physical harm if she didn't walk away from Cole, and then she'd dangled the carrot of her mother's supposed whereabouts.

Caroline wasn't stupid. She'd known the one thing most likely to make Brianna comply and had included Scottie in her threats. The only other people of significance to Brianna were Cole and Tyler. Since Caroline wanted Cole to herself she wasn't going to do anything to harm him, but she hated Tyler. As

Cole's best friend, Caroline might see him as being in the way, and therefore she might try to mess with him too.

Brianna snorted. Tyler could probably take Caroline with both arms tied behind his back.

Brianna sighed as she slipped the white silky material off the hanger and over her head. Of course it fit her perfectly, making her look like a prom queen. Or a bride, whichever.

However, even the allure of feeling like a princess couldn't keep the thoughts from running through her head. How had Caroline gotten information about her mother?

* * *

Cole strode through the boutique's door, uncaring about the noise he made or the stares he received. He had to see her, had to make sure for himself she was all right. When Tyler had called him, interrupting his meeting with his board of directors, it was all he could do not to drop the phone and run out.

Instead, he'd gruffly rescheduled the meeting, his heart pounding with a mixture of anxiousness and fear. Two emotions he couldn't remember ever feeling over a woman. Bri had changed him in the few short days she'd been with them, and he couldn't wait to make her his, permanently.

He scanned the room, looking for any sign of Tyler or Bri, and saw neither. Damn, he'd told Tyler he'd meet them here. Besides, Ty's car was still outside. Cole threw his hands on his hips and let out the breath he didn't realize he'd been holding. He was just about to start toward the back when a pint-sized pixie of a woman with a nametag reading Belle stepped in front of him, almost becoming a speed bump.

"Is there anything I can help you with?" She peeked at him from beneath her eyelashes.

"I'm looking for my fiancée and her bodyguard. I was supposed to meet them here."

The lady gulped and tried to be surreptitious about scanning the store. Her face flamed a telltale red, and Cole knew without a doubt Tyler had fucked Bri. Probably in the dressing room. Right about now, Belle was trying to figure out how to tell him his fiancée had just gotten it on with said bodyguard. Cole smiled. He could have put her out of her misery, but it would be a lengthy explanation of a threesome, and the look on her face was priceless.

"She's um..."

"Cole."

He glanced up to see Tyler bearing down on them, then back to the woman, whose face had gone an even darker red. "Thank you for your help. There he is now."

"But..."

Cole stepped around her, wondering if she'd ever encountered a more difficult situation. It was bad enough to know what your customers were doing behind the dressing room door, another thing altogether to realize the woman was fucking her bodyguard behind her fiancé's back. Cole laughed.

"Feel better, Ty?"

"One hundred percent." His face didn't even flush.

"Yeah, well, I'll let you explain to the clerk what was going on back there."

Tyler snorted. "I don't have to explain anything to her."

"What the fuck's going on, Ty? I drove over here like a bat out of hell and find out you and Bri are screwing each other in the dressing room." There had to be more to the story. Tyler had not sounded like himself during their phone call, and he would never have insisted they meet somewhere had nothing happened.

"That damn letter is what's going on," Ty snapped.

Cole followed him to a corner of the boutique where they could see both the front door and the dressing rooms.

"We went to Tonio's for lunch, apparently she goes there a lot by the way, and she's all fidgety. I couldn't get her to even look at me because she kept looking around for someone else. Finally she tells me about this note. Someone threatened her, Cole, and my money's on Caroline."

Caroline? "Sonofabitch." If there had been a decent wall next to him, he'd have punched his fist through it. No one messed with their woman. No one.

Tyler nodded, apparently agreeing with the direction of his thoughts. "She practically accosted Bri at the restaurant."

"What the hell was she doing there?"

Ty shrugged. "Don't know, but she came out of the bathroom just as I was going in, hissing and spitting like the she-bitch she is, and I find Bri in there sagging against the counter like someone had just killed her puppy."

"Did Caroline touch her?" Cole's breath hitched in his chest as he voiced his question with deadly menace.

"Not that I could see. All Bri would tell me is Caroline said she had information about her mother."

"Damn. How could she? You couldn't even get *your* hands on that."

"I don't know but—"

"Stop him. Thief." The small saleswoman shouted and pointed as she ran toward the front of the store. A man dressed in black pushed through the door and was gone before Cole or Tyler could focus their attention on what was happening, but both took off to stop Belle from pursuing the robber.

* * *

Brianna smoothed the sheer, silky fabric of the floaty skirt down her thighs, reveling in the feel against her legs. The dress made her look like an angel. She bent to put on the strappy sandals the saleswoman had just delivered. The door clicked behind her and she wondered for which one of her men she was putting on a show of her naked ass. The dress wasn't long enough to cover her when she was bent in half the way she was. The breeze along the slit of her globes could attest to that.

"I wish I had time to fuck that pretty cunt of yours, bitch."

Her heart stopped. A scream welled up in her, but the gruff hand seizing her throat prevented any noise from escaping. Red spots danced in her vision as her airway was blocked, her lungs seized.

The big man forcibly hauled her to a standing position. With his hand wrapped tight around her neck, he slammed the side of her face into the mirrored wall. The exact wall where Tyler had just made love to her. The jarring impact of her forehead cracked the glass in twenty different directions, giving her twenty different views of her attacker.

"Where's your money?" he grunted.

His breath was foul, like onions and cigars. She gasped, unable to comprehend what he wanted. He held her cheek smashed against the mirror, his fingers squeezing painfully. She couldn't have answered him if she'd wanted to. A dark blob grew before her eyes and her chest tightened in attack mode. If he held her much longer, she'd pass out.

What would happen then? Would he rape her? Would Tyler hear him, come looking for her? God, she didn't want him to see her like this. She wouldn't be able to face either one of them ever again. She would fight with everything in her before letting this man have her.

Except he had her pinned to the mirror, her arms squished harshly between her body and the glass. In the broken shards, she saw his eyes, light brown against the black facemask that covered everything else. He shifted behind her, allowing the tiniest bit of freedom for her arms, and she was able to twist one out of its confinement. It gave her strength over the unconscious state looming in the very near future. She wanted to speak, to tell him there was no money, but instead she croaked. Her throat was too jammed to allow her voice box to work.

"Shut the fuck up, bitch."

The gleaming edge of a knife glittered in the broken mirror as he brought it to her face and caressed her cheek with it. No! She would not die this way.

Deep inside, she found the strength to strike back. How she did it she would never know, but somehow she caught him off guard and smashed back at him with her freed fist. The shallow blow glanced off his nose, but it was all she needed. He loosed his hold on her neck to grab his face where blood was trickling out of one nostril. The other still held the knife but in an instant she was able to both swing around to face him and scream with everything she had.

His eyes went wide beneath the mask, and he lashed out at her with the knife. Brianna dove to the side, throwing her arms out as she tried to deflect the blade, but it caught her anyway. The cold steel bit through the silk material like it was melted butter and into her skin along her ribs with the same efficiency.

She fell to her knees and grasped the cut with the palm of her hand, immediately feeling the stickiness oozing through her fingers.

"Tyler," she screamed again and again, not sure if she was really making any noise at all, her throat hurt so much.

"You fucking bitch." The man above her looked around wildly before plunging back out the door and disappearing.

⁂ ⁂ ⁂

The scream pierced the soft music and attempted robbery confusion filling the store. Cole's heart stopped beating and his stomach dropped. A glance at Tyler told him his best friend was having the same reaction.

They knew that scream, though they'd never heard it laced with the fear it now was.

Cole and Tyler were running before her heart-wrenching scream ceased. The urgency of Bri's cry made Cole's gut twist and fear for her safety poured through him.

Tyler turned the corner one step ahead of him and slammed into a human wall, causing Cole to barrel into his back. They fell forward in a heap of arms and legs. As they went down, Cole glanced up, in what seemed like slow motion, to see a man, his stunned eyes glowing beneath a black mask. The man's arms windmilled as he tried to keep his feet, but with one step, he backed away and out of the reach of Tyler's outstretched arms. Then he shot off toward the back entrance.

Cursing, Cole rolled off Tyler and sprang to his feet. "You take him." He may as well have spoken to the air because Tyler was already up and sprinting after the man, his gun drawn, precious seconds separating them.

His heart pounding, Cole pushed open the first door he came to. Empty. A door slammed at the rear of the store.

There was a soft whimper to his left and through the crack of the next door, he saw an unmoving pool of white. He had to swallow back the panic threatening to claw its way up his throat.

"Cole?" Her voice was shaky, but she was alive, thank God.

The white mass of silk turned a crimson red the further he opened the door.

"Son of a bitch." He knelt beside Bri, who was also kneeling, and took in the pallor of her skin, the dilation of her pupils and the wheezing of her breath. "Where's your inhaler?" It was all he could do not to shout. His panicked fear had just taken a turn to fucking outrage.

"He cut me, Cole."

Her pained words cut him to the core. "Yeah, baby." *But where?* He'd kill the man if Tyler didn't first. There was the skirt she'd worn. He dug into the pocket and pulled out the inhaler, giving her a puff while he fumbled with his phone and called 911, quietly asking for paramedics.

"He said he wanted money."

I'll just fucking bet he did. "Shh, don't talk." She was shocked enough as it was, he didn't want to add to her problems. He laid the phone down next to them, open so dispatch could still hear him.

Belle tripped into the doorway. "Oh my God, is she okay?"

"No," he barked, forgetting his mission to be calm. Bri jumped beneath him, and he rubbed a hand down his face. "Go and wait for the police."

"Yes, sir."

Cole reached for Bri's hand hovering protectively over the left side of her rib cage.

"Don't yell at her, Cole."

"Don't scare me to death then. Let me see how bad it is." He pried her hand away. "Easy, baby," he cooed when she hissed.

"Hurts."

"I know." He turned and yelled out the door. "Get me some towels."

"You were scared?"

His fingers stilled and his gaze flew to hers. "Hell yeah. How could you ask that?"

She shrugged and winced as the action pulled at her wound. "It's just that..." She paused and closed her eyes.

"Hey."

Her eyes flew open. "What."

"You look like you're about to pass out on me." He ripped the dress off her shoulder, exposing her breast and the cut just to the left of it. "Damn. You're bleeding pretty good here." There was about a three-inch-long gash running along her ribs, a flesh wound, and not a puncture. At least the bastard had only been able to slice her, not stab her.

He hated the thought of having to hurt her anymore, but he was going to have to put pressure on the cut to try and stop the bleeding. He tore at his dress shirt, popping buttons off and yanking the tails out of his waistband. After wadding it up, he pressed it against her side.

Cole tried to ignore her groan of pain, but damn it, it made him hurt too. "Keep talking to me, baby. Why wouldn't I be scared?"

"Because...you...I thought maybe...I was just another conquest for you guys."

He stared hard at her, his body tense. "I love you." He relaxed a fraction when a ghost of a smile touched her lips.

"Tyler said the same thing."

"Then believe it, neither of us has ever said that to a woman before. If I have to spend the rest of my life proving it to you, I will. We will."

"It hasn't even been four days."

"So what."

The door behind him smashed against the wall. Cole guessed it wasn't open enough for Ty to get in, although it had been almost all the way open.

"Fucking bastard got away." Tyler was out of breath. "Ambulance just pulled up." He dropped to his knees and twisted his fingers with Bri's bloody ones. "How bad is it?"

"He sliced her. One more inch and he would have punctured a lung."

"Son of a bitch. He had to have been waiting for me to leave the room. He was good, I never saw anyone following us."

"He was after money," Brianna said.

"Get everyone you can on this," Cole growled, ignoring Bri's attempt to justify the situation.

"Already one step ahead of you." Tyler placed his hand on top of Cole's, adding his strength for pressure.

"It was a robbery," Brianna whispered.

"Did you get a description?" Cole said, overlooking Bri's soft interjection yet again.

Tyler nodded. "Sure. Caucasian, about five-ten, black mask, black clothes, and fast as hell."

"Not much to go on."

Bri coughed beneath them. "He wanted my money, guys."

"No, but I'd bet anything Caroline might know something. Like I said, she wasn't too happy to see me at Tonio's today."

"I can't see her doing something like this." Cole saw Tyler nod, but knew his friend wasn't convinced of his answer.

Blood was still oozing from beneath the shirt both of them held and Bri grimaced when they increased the pressure. "Sorry, baby," Cole soothed as she shook her head like she was shaking off the pain.

"Caroline? Guys," she shouted.

Both of them looked down into her face.

"The jelly here is trying to tell you this was a robbery."

"What have we got here?"

Two EMT's and a policeman were standing in the doorway.

"Knife wound along her ribs. A few inches long," Tyler answered.

"He said he w-wanted money." Bri was getting paler.

"You're going to have to clear the room so we can get to her." One of the medics leaned in and laid a hand on Tyler's shoulder. Cole stared at Ty.

"Fine, I'll go. You're gonna be okay, little one. I'll be right outside the door."

"Good." She nodded. "Great. Give me your shirt first."

"What?"

"Your shirt, Ty, I'm just a teeny bit exposed here, thanks to Cole, in case you hadn't noticed."

Tyler growled. "I wouldn't be a man if I hadn't noticed. I wouldn't be a gentleman if I'd done something about it."

She snorted and his eyebrows shot up. "There's nothing gent-gentleman about you, Ty."

He conceded defeat and stripped out of the T-shirt, then covered her exposed breast with it. "She's got asthma, keep an eye on it," he warned before stepping out of the room.

Cole heard Tyler's discussion with the police in the periphery of his brain.

"Cole." Sweat had broken out on her upper lip as the EMT's looked at her wound. "It wasn't her, Cole. It was a robbery."

"Maybe." Ty had him thinking now though. "This *is* too much of a coincidence, Bri. The same day she threatens you, you get attacked?" He'd talk to Caroline later and find out more.

"We're ready to transport. We'll start an IV in the ambulance."

Cole nodded. "I'm going with you."

"Sorry, you'll have to follow."

"Like hell, I will." Apparently they'd heard him outside because an officer peeked his head in.

"This is Cole Masters. I think you can make an exception for him."

"I'm sorry. It'll be a tight fit, but somehow we'll squeeze you in."

Normally, Cole hated throwing his name around, but this was one instance where he had no qualms using it.

"Cole, just follow. I'll be fine."

He looked into her pain-laced blue eyes. "Forget it. Someone just tried to kill you. I'm not leaving you alone for one minute." He turned to the group of police and spoke to Tyler. "We're going to St. Michael's."

Tyler raised a hand before tucking it back under his armpit. "I'm giving these guys about two more minutes, then they're going to have to follow me there."

"Yeah, right."

* * *
** ** **

It was dark when they finally got home. Cole had asked Freddy to drop off some clothes for all of them and his car, so at least he'd been able to bring her home when it was time. Tyler had stopped by and stayed for a good hour, but then he'd taken off after seeing Bri was going to be fine. He was scheduled to meet with Bri's father tonight to discuss a few things about their arrangement.

Cole had seen how much it hurt Tyler for him to have to leave her the way things were. His eyes had been filled with both hatred and anxiety. The same things Cole was feeling. Now, as the adrenaline wore off, he began to see things a little clearer. He had no doubt Tyler would find whoever was behind the attack on Bri. If it was Caroline, she was going to be sorry she'd ever laid eyes on Cole.

With a sigh, he got out and rounded the hood of the SUV. He opened the back door to find Bri lying on her good side, her eyes closed. She was wearing a pair of green scrubs a nurse had rounded up for them at the hospital. They were about two sizes too big on her slender frame, but at least he hadn't hurt her much when he'd helped shove her arms into the sleeves. He would never have been able to do that with the shirt Freddy had brought for her. He didn't even know where the man had found it.

One arm dangled toward the floor, a shoe clutched in her fist. He smiled at the image she presented.

Somehow he managed to gently tug her into a sitting position and lift her out of the car.

She hummed against his throat, practically purring. "Mmm. You smell sooo good."

Cole cradled her slight weight to keep from pulling on her side where she'd just gotten sixteen stitches to repair the knife wound. It hadn't been as severe as the amount of blood had led them to believe, but no way would he let the size of the cut keep him from wanting to kill the bastard who did this to her.

He'd paled every time the doctor had placed a stitch, and gotten warned more than once to sit down before he fainted. He winced every time she half-consciously groaned, and tried really hard not to punch the doctor who'd patched her up. In retrospect he'd been hurting more than she had, with the painkillers they'd given her.

He adjusted her in his grip when she kicked her leg out, nearly unbalancing them. A bare foot, complete with pink-painted toenails, attracted his attention. *I wonder if she's still got the other shoe.* Maybe that's what she'd been talking to in the back of his SUV.

Five minutes into the trip, he'd given up trying to make sense out of her conversation. She, on the other hand, had chatted very happily to whatever she could see. Very happily. Cole grinned despite the seriousness of the situation then froze mid-stride, his body hardening to the point of pain in a nanosecond.

"You taste good too," she whispered as she licked him with a delicate, velvet tongue just under his jaw.

The little kitty was lapping him up. Blood roared in his ears and his cock, thickening his length into what felt like abnormal proportions. He envisioned laying her out on the steps, belly down, and taking her from behind, the globes of her ass flushing beneath his hands.

She's hurt. Hurt, hurt, hurt. He repeated the mantra, demanding his cock into obedience. There would be no sex now, or for the rest of the night. Pain meds or no. The most he could do, and would do, is hold her and convince himself she was really still alive.

He twisted his head, stretching his neck away from her wandering tongue. "Sweetheart, Bri, baby. Stop that." His fingers itched to swat her behind for egging him into this state of hypersensitivity, but to do so he'd have to put her down. Wasn't gonna happen.

He sighed. "Let's get you inside and into bed, baby."

The skin of his throat tingled beneath the raspberry she blew on it. "Don't want to."

He laughed at her petulant tone but sighed again when she reached up and patted the air next to what he supposed she thought was his cheek. He took the steps two at a time, barely jarring Bri as he bounded up them. The front door opened before they hit the top.

"How is she?" Scottie stood in the doorway, a slightly belligerent force to be reckoned with.

For a second, Cole wondered if the kid would hold him and Tyler responsible. The thought riding close on those coattails was, why wouldn't he? Cole held himself liable for not sticking by the door of the dressing room with a bazooka in his hand. The scenario might be a little farfetched, but at least the bastard would have thought twice about trying to rape and kill the woman who tomorrow would be their wife.

He shifted Bri again, when her body suddenly went limp. Only the steady rise and fall of her chest against his kept his mind from wandering in a forbidden direction. His little nymph had finally gone to sleep.

"Sixteen stitches, and just a tiny bit loony."

Scott cocked his head and grinned, and Cole's lungs deflated on the breath that whooshed out in his relief. The last thing he wanted was Bri upset because Scott was angry with him and Tyler.

"A tiny bit?" Scott snorted as he scooted back and allowed Cole to enter his own home.

Brianna nuzzled further into Cole, heavy sleep dragging her down.

"Brianna can't even handle extra-strength Tylenol, I can imagine what she's been like on a real pain pill," Scott continued.

"I believe she was talking to her shoe."

The kid spit out a laugh then covered his mouth with his hand, his eyes twinkling. "That wasn't funny was it?"

"The part where your sister got stabbed? No, not funny at all. The shoe bit? Pretty damned funny." Cole started up the staircase, not even feeling the weight of Bri in his arms. He would never get enough of holding her close like this. Scott kept up with them. His talent for moving around in his dark world still amazed Cole.

"What's going to happen now?"

There was a tiny, scared twinge in Scott's voice, which pulled at Cole. "We're getting married."

"Good."

"Good?" Cole hadn't expected Scott's instant acceptance to his announcement. Actually, he'd thought Bri's brother might throw a punch or two, or at the very least put up a protest.

"Well yeah, for you and her. I don't think Andrew Wyatt will like it too much. You're screwing up his plans."

"I don't give a shit what your fath...Andrew Wyatt thinks. She's mine." He turned to open the door with the hand he had wrapped around Bri's back. Scott got to it first, unerringly finding the knob and opening the door. Cole felt his jaw drop. "Are you sure you can't see."

Scott smiled and ducked his head, a dull red creeping into his cheeks. "Absolutely."

"I'm not even gonna ask how you do some of the things you do," Cole said, laying Bri gently on his side of the bed. On the other side, he peeled the sheets back. Then he collected her again, wincing when she moaned through her deep sleep and the medication. So help her God, if Caroline had anything to do with this, he'd wring her neck.

"I'm all good with you guys getting married. I'd like to see my sister truly happy for once." His face turned toward the window as if he were gazing out at the valley lying below and he muttered, "You guys make her that way, but *she* may not be too excited about it. Did you ask her, or tell her?"

Cole shook his head. "No, I didn't ask, and why wouldn't she want to?"

Scott stuck a finger in the air. "A, she's a woman. Don't they get all pissy if you tell instead of ask? Two, she may balk at only knowing you for four days, again, a woman thing, and tres, the first thing out of her mouth is going to be, 'I won't do that to Scottie. My father would have him put away.'"

Cole propped his hands on his hips, disbelief ringing through him. "How do you know all this? When I was sixteen the only things I thought about were girls and, well, girls."

Scott smiled again. "You don't live in the same world I live in."

"Obviously not." Cole snorted and swiped a hand over his face. The kid was right. Those would be the first words out of Bri's mouth. He slapped his palm on his thigh and hoped to hell Tyler was having good luck with her father. Then there would be absolutely nothing preventing her from marrying them. Okay, the four days he couldn't do anything about, but it was enough for him to know he wanted to spend the rest of his life with her.

"Scott..." Cole thumped him on the back of his shoulder as he guided them out of the bedroom, "...how would you like living here permanently?"

Chapter Nine

Brianna moaned and buried her head deeper into her pillow. How long had she slept? An hour, all night? She peeked with one eye and blinked at the bright rays of light spilling through the bedroom window. Must be morning. She closed her eye. A few more minutes, then she'd get up. She tried to roll onto her side but was stopped by a hand on her shoulder. She smiled.

"Stay," Tyler whispered, his hand trailing across her chest to settle on her breast. He kneaded the fleshy mound, palming the softened peak until Brianna felt it harden into a tight point. "Keep your eyes closed, little one." His breath was warm on her ear, his tongue wet as it lapped out to taste the lobe, sending shivers over her naked skin.

She arched her back as another pair of hands spread her thighs, drawing her knees up just slightly. Her breath caught in anticipation of Cole touching her. She clenched her pussy together, silently begging for him to.

"Let us love you, baby." Cole's lips tickled her entrance as he spoke.

"Aah." She arched again, then froze at the semi-painful tug at her side reminding her of the events of yesterday. Brianna was paralyzed, her entire body stiffened until her back hurt and her stitches ached. She panted and squeezed her eyes tight trying to stave off the images of the man who'd attacked her.

"Relax, little one. He can't hurt you anymore. You're safe, we're here."

They were right. Nothing would happen here in their bedroom. Nothing she didn't want to happen anyway. The soft mattress conformed to her body as she sank back into it. It just as quickly released her as she shot upward with the swipe of Cole's tongue along her slit. She hissed at another slight pull along her side and thanked the lucky stars her pain meds hadn't worn off completely.

Tyler's mouth opened on her nipple, sucking it tightly into its warmth and tugging in sync with Cole's mouth on her clit. The twin sensations had Brianna at her peak within seconds, but not over. They were relentless with their tongues. Ty's moved between her nipples, licking and sucking, then biting down until she screamed out with the pleasure/pain.

"Please." She writhed in the sheets. *Just a little more, a little harder. Damn it!*

"Please, what, baby? What do you need?" Cole's tongue dove into her pussy, drawing her moisture out where he spread it with his fingertips.

"God." Her head could not tilt back any farther without breaking her neck. She dug her heels in, ignoring the twinge of pain again, too caught up with the tiny sparks of heat thrumming through her body to care, and tried to force herself closer to both their mouths. "More, just more, please," she gritted out.

Cole's finger slid through her cream and glided from her exposed clit, through her drenched folds, across the sensitive skin of her perineum, and ended up circling the opening of her ass. His tongue speared into her again, plunging in and out, but it wasn't enough. Not nearly enough. She groaned and tossed her head back and forth on the pillow.

"Maybe if you thought about something else," Ty murmured. He left her nipples, leaving them aching with need.

"No, don't leave." She cried and bit her lip, then replaced his fingers with her own. She pulled and pinched each of the beaded tips.

"Oh, I'm not leaving. That's it, touch yourself." The bed dipped beside her head and she opened her eyes to the sight of Ty's groin, his rigid cock stiff and begging for attention. "Suck it, Bri." His growled words alerted her to his near loss of control, and her mouth watered.

Brianna took his length into her mouth just as Cole breached her back entrance with two slick fingers. She lifted her head, lodging the plum-shaped head of Ty's penis at the back of her throat, gagging her until she overcame the sensation and breathed around him.

Ty moved then, shifting his hips and pulling almost all the way out before smoothly thrusting back in.

"That's it, little one, lick me."

Cole's fingers worked her ass, stretching her as his tongue stroked her vagina. One touch to her swollen clit and she'd explode. But then, he knew that. The bastard was just drawing it out, waiting for her to scream in frustration before he let her come.

Her nipples stung beneath her tweaking fingers, zinging the sensations straight to her womb. She flexed her vaginal walls, encompassing Cole's tongue and trying to trap him there, deep inside her.

Her lips cramped around Tyler's thickness as she savored the musky taste of his sex. She scraped her teeth along the prominent vein running underneath the length of his dick and swirled her tongue over the soft head. She licked along the slit with the tip of her tongue and tasted his pre-come as he slowly fucked her mouth.

"Is she ready?" Tyler's jaw was tight when she looked up the length of his chest to his upturned face. A drop of sweat rolled off his chin and fell with a soft plop on her cheek.

"Hell yeah," Cole murmured.

His tongue stopped dipping into her channel and Brianna cried out. She lifted her hips, trying to recapture his mouth, nearly dislodging the fingers still wreaking havoc in her backside.

Then those magical fingers were gone too and she heard him laugh as he shifted between her legs and entered her pussy to the hilt with one long, slow thrust. Her eyes watered, her mouth tightened on Tyler's cock, causing him to growl, and she moaned as the muscles between her legs contracted around Cole's cock. Finally, she had him right where she wanted him. Both of them.

"I can't wait," Cole grunted.

"Like you fucking think I can?" Ty barked back.

"Mm eetha," she panted through her full mouth.

"I don't want to hurt you, baby." Cole slid his fingers gently over her bandage-covered stitches as he held himself immobile inside her.

Brianna yanked her lips off Tyler's penis and glared at Cole. Her heart was racing, her breath bellowing out of her lungs, her clit was primed to shoot off like a rocket, and he didn't want to hurt her?

"You can't...please...move. Something. Don't do this to me," she demanded. "I'm not...you're not hurting me."

Something in her eyes must have clued him in. He reached a hand between their bodies and stoked her clit in tiny circles.

"Yesss." Her head fell back in ecstasy. *More, more.*

Tyler turned her face toward his cock and reinserted himself in her open mouth. She moaned around his length.

"Screw it." Cole withdrew and slid home, setting up a rhythm that had Tyler moving with them just to stay in her mouth.

Cole placed one hand on the bed beside her shoulder, opposite of Tyler, to anchor himself. His other hand still played wickedly at her clit. She was so close, but she needed more. Needed him to move faster, harder.

Brianna raised her hips, urging him to do so. Cole took the hint, increasing his tempo several degrees and finally creating the stronger friction she craved.

"So fucking tight. I'm not gonna last, baby," he hissed.

Stars burst behind her eyelids when she closed them to capture each sensation of his cock sucking in and out of her. Three more strokes were all Cole could handle. She felt his balls slap against her rear one last time as he buried himself inside her so there wasn't a lick of space between them. Hot pulses of his come jetted into her, flooding her pussy and sparking off her own explosion as it splashed into her womb.

Tyler continued to pump into her mouth, using his hand at the base of his cock as a guide so in his lust-filled frame of mind he wouldn't force her to take too much. She laid a hand on a hair-roughened thigh and felt it stiffen beneath her palm. His chest rumbled, his body tensed completely and he covered the back of her throat with his release.

She swallowed him again and again, milking Tyler's cock with her tongue and Cole's still pulsing one with her vagina.

Sweat coated the three of them as they sat, suspended in their aftermath. Tyler was bent over her, his penis softening in her mouth as she licked it softly. Cole too was bent over her, the other direction, rocking gently against her clit. They panted in time with each other, their bodies slick and sticking together wherever they touched.

⁑ ⁑ ⁑

"We're getting married." Cole placed the plate of food in front of Bri's seat at the kitchen island. The lump on her forehead where the bastard had smashed her head into the mirror was a gross shade of purple. Tyler sat to her right, chugging on a Coke and digging into a bowl of canned raviolis.

Bri choked on the tea she'd just taken a drink of, earning a thump on the back from Ty.

"What?" she gasped when she caught her breath.

The look on her face was priceless. Her eyebrows had disappeared behind her bangs, and her eyes were as wide as quarters.

After recovering from their mid-morning loving, Bri had slept again, tucked between both he and Ty, safe. He hadn't meant to take her, only to give her pleasure, release from the stress of yesterday. But then she'd begged and neither he nor Tyler could have walked away.

He'd checked her stitches while she slept, relieved beyond belief they hadn't hurt her further by aggravating her side with their wild fucking.

"This afternoon. We're getting married," he repeated as she sat there trying not to sputter.

"Why?"

"Why?" Cole raised an eyebrow when she looked at him like he were some kind of bug. "Why else. I love you."

"Ditto," Tyler said around a mouthful of ravs.

"And someone tried to attack you yesterday," Cole continued, not bothering to mention Caroline's name. Tyler was busy trying to track her down and get some answers. There was no sense in upsetting Bri any further, especially when he knew she would deny the possibility anyway.

"I was there, remember?" Her face fell, reddening with embarrassment or anger or both. "But that has nothing to do with a proposal, or statement in your case, of marriage, Cole. We've known each other for five days."

"Do you love us?" he asked. "Would it matter if we'd known each other for four years?"

"Yes."

Cole smiled. "Yes to which question?"

She slumped in her chair. "Damn you, you know which one."

His heart thumped. Armed with the knowledge she loved him, maybe he wouldn't have to reveal part of the reason for his wanting to marry her so quickly. He certainly didn't want her thinking the only reason was for her protection. She'd never go for that, and he didn't have time to woo her for months if she did.

Tyler turned in his seat and took hold of her hand, pulling it into his lap where he caressed it with his fingertips. "You'll be safer with his name attached to yours, Bri."

Well, there went the idea of not telling her the most pressing reason for marriage.

"Safer? From what?"

Cole cleared his throat, agitated by the fact she could downplay everything that had happened to her. How could she still think yesterday had been a simple robbery?

"I was robbed in a store, Cole, mugged."

She did. He shook his head. "That was no mugging, Bri. There were two men there. One in the front who distracted us while the other one targeted you in the back. You were set up." His gut clenched when her face drained of color. He heard her swallow despite the clinking of Tyler's spoon against his bowl.

"I didn't know that," she whispered and pulled her hand out of the one Tyler still gripped her with.

She sat for long seconds and he let her, wanting it to sink in that she really did have a problem. Her spine straightened and she looked at him.

"I still can't marry you." Her hands shook as she reached for her glass.

Tyler dropped his spoon to the table and jerked his gaze to her. Cole settled his hips against the island next to her chair and crossed his arms over his chest. He looked down at the top of her head.

"Why not."

"Scottie."

Damn the kid, pulling his all-knowledgeable crap. He'd called this one. She still didn't know about him staying with them when this was all over. She'd been asleep last night when Tyler had finally gotten home, and then this morning...well, other things had come up. Like his and Tyler's dicks when they'd awoken to her naked, sleep-induced-aroused body, flushed from whatever dream she was having.

"What about him?"

"My father would be so pissed, he'd have him taken away from me, that's what."

Cole grinned, relaxing with the news he had for her. "Taken care of, baby."

"What do you mean?" she said, suspiciousness lacing her voice.

"I went last night and got your father to sign over guardianship of Scott to Cole. He's staying here with us. Andrew gave up all rights to his son with one swipe of his pen," Tyler said. He leaned back and hooked his hand around the nape of her neck, squeezing at a place where Cole suspected she had a knot.

"I don't believe it." Bri jumped from her seat and stared at Tyler.

"Believe it, little one, I was there, as was Cole's lawyer, and your father's lawyer. There were lots of witnesses. It can't be disputed because I even had it signed by a judge."

Her eyes were shiny and darted between Tyler and himself. Was she happy? Scared? He wondered what was going on inside her head. She swallowed again and Cole ducked his chin to hide his smile.

"How did you do all that in one night?"

"Money talks, Bri." Cole shrugged when she looked at him incredulously. "I'm the first to admit I don't use my money to make people jump through hoops, but I will do anything for you. Anything." He reached a hand out and grabbed her wrist, tugging her to him and tucking her head carefully beneath his chin to avoid the bruises.

"Of course, it helped when Cole told Andrew he wouldn't touch you until he signed the papers." Tyler settled back into his lunch. "Talk about jumping through hoops. That man would do anything Cole asked him to do, so long as he thinks he's going to get a baby out of the deal."

"Exactly." Her words were muffled against Cole's chest and she tried to pull away from him, but he held her in a loose, unbreakable hold. He rubbed circles on her back instead. "Did you tell him we were getting married?"

"No. That's none of his business. Was that a yes?"

She looked up at him then, her eyes bright with what he hoped was trust and desire. Not sexual, but a desire to want to stay with them forever.

"What will happen when he finds out? Provided I say yes, of course."

Cole inhaled. She was close, he just had to nudge her over the edge and she'd be theirs. "Nothing will happen. I haven't signed his contract, Bri. Any child we have will be ours. We are the parents, he would have no rights except those of a grandparent. If he wants a son of ours to inherit, so be it."

"God, could it be this simple?" she whispered, a fat tear dropping off an eyelash to splash on her pale cheekbone. She wrapped her arms around his back, hugging him the way he was her. Tyler came to stand behind her so she was sandwiched between them, wrapped in both their arms. Tyler leaned over, pushed her hair out the way with his chin and kissed the column of her neck.

"Yes it could," Tyler whispered to her. "If you let it."

She turned then, looking over her shoulder and sniffing. "How would this work? I don't think polygamy is allowed in the state of Missouri." She gave them both a shy smile and Cole knew he had her.

He echoed the words Tyler had said to him just yesterday. "It'll be you and me on paper, baby, Tyler in your heart. It's not like I want to be married to him. And besides," he winked at her, "it only has to be real to the three of us, not to anyone else."

She buried her head on his chest again and was silent. Then she nodded, moaning as her sore forehead rubbed against his shirt.

Cole lifted her face to his with his finger. "Are you saying yes, baby? I need the words."

"Yes."

She cried, long wet happy sobs soaking his shirt as Tyler rubbed her shoulders and kissed the side of her face.

Both of them squeezed her tight until she shrieked and threw a hand up protectively over her side. Shit. How could he have forgotten?

"You okay, little one?" Tyler got to his knees and peeled her tank top up to inspect her wound and make sure they hadn't split her stitches. He planted a few kisses to her side before standing.

"I'm fine." She laughed, all teary and snotty, and kissed them both on the cheek.

"Is it safe to come in, or are you guys doing something nasty I don't want to see?" Scott spoke from the doorway he was leaning against, smug smile stretched across his face.

"Very funny, Scottie. Don't want to see. I'll give you something you don't want to see."

"Did you ask yet?" He turned to Cole.

Amazing. "Yes."

"What'd she say?" His eyes glittered with laughter.

"Just what you said she would."

Scottie chuckled.

"Why did you already know about this, and what did you say I would say?" She crossed the room to take Scottie's arm and swatted him on the shoulder.

"That you would say no because of me, and I know about this because Cole told me yesterday while you were busy talking with your shoe."

She swatted him again with a "humph".

"Damn I wish I had seen this shoe incident." Tyler set his bowl in the sink after rinsing it out and headed for the door. The indignant Bri slapped him on the way.

She sat at the table and groaned. "I don't handle pain medication well, you asses."

Three male voices chuckled and responded, "We know."

✳ ✳ ✳

Brianna stared at herself in the mirror she'd found attached to the back of the judge's door, butterflies tickling her tummy. The grotesque bruise mottled her temple, spreading down to her cheekbone. No amount of makeup could completely cover it.

She was wearing a dress identical to the one she'd been attacked in, minus the rips and blood. It was Ty's favorite, and he wanted to see her wearing it on her wedding day.

Her wedding day. It was not going the way she had envisioned her dream day would go. There was no church brimming with friends and family, not that she had any, no flowers, no music and no reception hall to dance the night away. The only thing there definitely would be was a wedding night. Albeit with two grooms. *More meat for me.*

She smiled at herself. At no time in her life had she thought about being with two men at one time. Now she couldn't imagine it any other way. They'd each shared some fabulous one on one's, but G-O-D, the times when they were all together. Mmm-mmm.

"You're beautiful, little one."

Brianna spun around to see Tyler in the doorway, his hands behind his back. "Sheesh, you scared the hell out of me Ty."

"Sorry. I brought you these." He pulled his arms forward to reveal a bouquet of gorgeous tulips and lilies.

Flowers. He'd brought her flowers just when she was thinking nothing would be normal about her wedding. Her throat clogged and her eyes watered. She shouldn't have doubted either one of them would let her feel less than important today.

"Hey, what's wrong?"

He came toward her, holding the flowers in front of him. The tulips were white and pink, and the lilies, bright pink Stargazers. Scottie must have told them what her favorites were because he'd hit the nail on the head.

She shook her head. "Nothing," she burst out, unaware she'd been holding her breath.

He hugged her, pulling her into a strong, yet tender embrace and kissed her forehead, making her laugh. She had two very yummy, sexual men who adored her. What more could she ask for?

Scottie's safety, that's what. After Caroline's threatening words at Tonio's, Brianna couldn't help but be afraid for her brother. Her lungs seized in her chest, tightening and squeezing painfully. The elephant was back, something she experienced rarely in the arms of Cole and Tyler, where she felt free and truly happy for the first time in her life.

"Damn it, Bri, where's your inhaler?"

She pointed to the antique desk where she'd laid her bag when she'd been given this office to prepare for the ceremony.

"Sit down before you fall down."

Her breath wheezed in and out as she tried to force air through passageways which were closing themselves off. She sat in the leather armchair in front of the desk and put her arms in the air.

"Here." Tyler returned to her, holding the inhaler.

Thankfully he held it to her lips because she didn't think she could, the way her hands were shaking so much. She held the first puff with as deep a breath as she could draw and immediately felt the tension ease. A second puff had her collapsing in the chair in relief.

"Better, little one?" Tyler knelt in front of her and rubbed her thighs beneath the silky skirt.

His touch ignited something deep in her belly, warming her pussy. He smiled, the arrogant beast.

"We can't do that right now, you naughty girl," he said smugly. "You're about to get married."

Brianna dropped her head back and savored the feel of his hands on the sensitive skin of her inner thighs.

The door opened again. Scottie poked his head through the crack. "It's time."

"You ready, little one?" Tyler winked at her.

She nodded at him, then groaned. "Yes, we'll be right there, Scottie." He shut the door, a smirk splitting his face. She sighed and faced Ty.

"Ty, are you sure you're okay with this? I mean, with me marrying Cole." She was nervous all around. If she or Cole hurt Ty's feelings or made him feel like an outsider, she'd never be able to forgive herself.

"Cole and I have already talked about this, Bri. We're both good with the way things are going to be. I may not be able to wear a ring or introduce you as my wife, but," he took her hand and placed it over his chest, "in here, you'll always be mine too."

Her eyes watered. She loved them both so much. Unbelievable after knowing them for only half a week.

"Besides..." he continued, his eyes sparkling with mischief, "...what if I find a wife of my own someday?"

Brianna's mouth dropped open. Her heart pounded against her ribs. She hadn't even thought about that possibility. The loss of him in their bed would be monumental, because no way could she stand by and watch while he made love to another woman, let alone participate.

Her body shook with the image. *And how selfish is that?* Especially when he and Cole shared her with all their love. But they never touched each other, so asking her to be with another woman... No way, uh-uh.

"Don't think so much, Bri, you'll get a headache."

She snapped her jaw shut. "I wasn't...I... It's just..."

"Hey." He cupped the back of her head and grinned at her. "I'm not talking about you being with another woman."

She raised an eyebrow. He lifted one of his own right back at her.

"Because, as much as most men may fantasize about two chicks together, I assure you, I don't. Cole and I have been this way for a long time. It suits us both, makes us complete somehow, but I have never, nor will ever, want to touch him in a sexual way." He gave a mock shiver and winked at her. "Except when we're both inside of you."

Brianna slapped him on the shoulder.

"You're incorrigible."

"Ditto."

"Ugh."

"Come on, little one, let's go make you a wife."

* * *
** ** **

It seemed the ceremony was over before any of them could blink. Tyler stood with Bri on the steps of the marble justice building. He felt better having his SIG Sauer safely resting at the small of his back once again. Earlier he'd handed it and his permit to the guard, lest they not be admitted to the inner sanctum of the courthouse because of regulations.

"That went well," Tyler mumbled. Bri was quiet, almost subdued next to him. Who could blame her? She'd been through hell this week, being blackmailed and attacked. Then she married a man who, besides his sexual preferences, was a virtual stranger. Okay two men, he conceded, because like he'd told her earlier, he considered himself her husband in every way. He only hoped she did too.

To top it off, she'd gotten married in front of a judge and Scottie, who'd already taken off with their limo driver. Probably not the idea of every little girl's dream wedding. They'd change that, Ty promised himself. Just as soon as all this messy business was cleared up.

As of right now, they were no closer to knowing the identity of her attacker, though they strongly suspected Caroline was somehow behind it. He had tried to track her down after the incident in the boutique yesterday, but had come up empty. She had probably guessed that Bri would tell Cole what had happened in the restroom, and had wisely disappeared off the face of the Earth. Looking for an alibi, no doubt, biding her time until Cole's blood stopped boiling over her possessiveness. Surely the viper wasn't stupid enough to think they wouldn't catch her.

How many times had he tried to warn Cole about her? Now look what happened. She'd threatened Brianna like the selfish snob she was.

He hated the small amount of vulnerability not finding her presented.

Ty swung his gaze up and down the street. There was nothing unusual. There hadn't been yesterday either, and for the lapse in his judgment, he could shoot himself.

Bri shifted beside him with what seemed like anxiousness. "Where did Cole park anyway, East Bufu?" she asked.

"Seems like it," he granted. He'd been wondering that too. Maybe they should go back inside.

"There he is." Bri pointed at the same time Tyler spotted their ride.

"I see him."

Cole's black SUV turned the corner about two blocks up and Ty put his hand on Bri's back to usher her down the steps. They stopped at the curb and waited while Cole sat through a red light.

The hairs on the back of his neck tingled. He had his hand on the butt of his gun before the rev of an engine registered in his brain. The squeal of tires was exacerbated by a woman's shrill scream.

Ty turned and shielded Bri from the new threat.

"What's going on, Ty?" She laid a hand in the middle of his back and he reached back to tuck his arm around her body.

"Shit."

The dark sedan flew at them, scattering pigeons and screeching down the quarter panel of a pick-up truck parallel parked beside them. Tyler yanked Bri into the street, opposite the direction of the out-of-control car. His ankle twisted on the uneven pavement, sending shards of lightning up to his knee, and bringing both him and Bri down.

At the last second he rolled, protecting her body from the gritty pavement and the weight of his body. She screamed and covered her face with both hands as they twisted on the concrete.

The car jumped the curb, slamming into a parking meter and sending the metal top airborne. The engine hissed on a puff of steam at the grinding halt. The gears ground out and Ty's eyes widened.

The sedan's tires spun crazily, smoking and shrieking as they tried to find purchase. And then they did and the car shot off backward. The fender of the pick-up ripped off and clattered to the ground.

Tyler turned over and covered every inch of Bri's body with his own, jarring his ankle and making it scream in agony. He buried his face in her neck. The tears on his cheek were hot as she sobbed. People were screaming, a siren whined in the distance, and then there was more tire squealing.

A crowd gathered around them and pressed into them, bombarding them with questions. Were they all right, did they need an ambulance, did they see who it was? Tyler shook his head.

"Shh, little one, I've got you," he murmured, worried when her keening grew louder.

"He tried to kill us, Ty. Did you see that? He...he tried to run us down. Oh my God." She pushed at his chest only to pull him back in with her fists clenched in his dress shirt.

Her breath wheezed out of her lungs. Tyler fumbled in his pocket for her inhaler and forced her to take a puff when she jerked her head out of reach.

"Get the fuck out of the way."

Tyler looked up, squinting in the bright sunlight to see the angry charge of a bull named Cole shoving his way through the anxious crowd.

"I fucking lost him." He jabbed a hand in his hair making it stick out in all directions. "I barely got turned around to follow and he was gone." Cole knelt beside them. "Bri, baby, look at me, tell me you're all right."

She did and nodded but couldn't speak for the tears. Cole's hands traced her body, looking at old injuries and searching for new ones. He pulled her up so she was sitting, and hugged her, squeezing until she squeaked. Then he bent and kissed her, making sure she was really okay. He gripped her hand and helped her stand on her wobbly legs.

"I'm fine," she sniffed. Her whole body vibrated with tremors that shook Cole as he held her to him, his palm rubbing circles on her back.

Tyler knew a drop from an adrenaline rush like this one could be a bitch on the nervous system.

"Son-of-a-bitch. I didn't even get a chance to honk a warning and he was on you. I thought I was gonna lose you."

"Everybody okay here?" A mounted patrolman joined the group of onlookers. Everyone started talking to him at once, yelling and pointing.

Tyler just wanted to get Bri the hell out of there. He pushed to his knees and stood. The pain in his ankle made him double over. It wasn't broken, he was sure, just sprained, but goddamn, it hurt like a mother.

"You hurt, Ty?"

"No," he said, shaking his head. "Just twisted my damn ankle when we stepped off."

Cole nodded, content with his answer for now. "Let's get her in the cab so I can take a closer look at those stitches."

"I'll give the cop our names and a sit-rep and tell him to call us later for details."

"Good idea." Cole looked both ways along the street just to make sure before he led Bri to the SUV and stowed her in the back seat. He followed her in and shut the world out. Ty knew Cole would take good care of her, he just hated being the one to have put her in danger yet again.

They had one more day to get through. Tomorrow night was the party where Cole would announce his marriage to Bri. Caroline was bound to show her face and since she didn't know about the wedding, she was going to be pissed. Then they would have her, because he could almost guarantee the bitch would start spouting things once she learned the truth and saw the rock on Bri's finger.

Tyler wiped at a patch of blood beading on his elbow beneath his ripped sleeve and made a vow.

They *would* catch this slime. And she would pay.

Chapter Ten

Friday night had come too soon. Brianna twisted her hands together and willed her stomach to settle. There were enough people at Cole's party to hold a democratic convention.

The sunken ballroom was decked out with flickering white lights and beautiful greenery. Massive flower arrangements adorned each corner of the spacious room where guests mingled in their formalwear. But she was only concerned about one.

Since Cole had already invited Caroline, he was expecting her to show up. The number of undercover security guards swarming the party was true testimony to how strongly he suspected Caroline of having something to do with the attacks. He thought if Caroline could see once and for all she would never get him, she would back off. Brianna still had her doubts though. The whole thing was like something out of a romance novel, complete with jilted lover.

Scottie was Brianna's main concern. She had a feeling when Caroline was confronted with the marriage, there was no way the woman would simply back off. Not according to their conversation in Tonio's restaurant. If Caroline came in spewing her filth and doing something to jeopardize her brother's welfare, Brianna would strangle her.

A warm hand traced small circles on the exposed skin of her back. "Relax, baby, take a deep breath."

Easy for you to say. She gritted her teeth and tried to think of something that wouldn't tip him off in the direction of her real thoughts. "It's hard to relax when you're touching me, Cole." She turned to him with a sickly sweet smile he instantly saw through.

He snorted and moved behind her, wrapping his arms around her and displaying his possessiveness. He may as well have taken her breasts in both his hands the way he was holding her. Her cheeks flamed.

I'm used to this, he's done it all week. Just not in front of two hundred people.

Her tummy dropped again. She'd never been in front of so many people. Neither had Scottie. Where was he? She stood on her tiptoes and tried to look over the throng of people.

"He's fine, Bri." Cole's breath tickled her neck just before his tongue darted out and teased along the cartilage at the top of her ear. "He's with Ty over at the bar."

Damn it. How could he read her so well after only one week, and please God, why wouldn't he stop doing what he was doing before she melted in front of all these people or did something really embarrassing? "Yeah, well I can't see him."

He chuckled as she squirmed to dodge his roving tongue. "He's there, I promise. I think they're trying to get my brother to play a little golf later."

That statement was all it took. Brianna let her troubles slide and rested her head against Cole's chest. If he wanted to take care of all her insecurities tonight, she'd gladly let him.

Behind her, Cole cleared his throat and straightened, alerting Brianna. "Don't look now, but here comes dear, old daddy."

She groaned and reached for her renewed queasy stomach once again. Scottie was safe, away from his clutches, but her father still didn't know she'd married Cole. They had agreed upon using the party tonight to tell him, knowing he would be furious. She reminded herself about the tight security. There would be plenty should things get out of hand with either her father or Caroline. The chief of police was even in attendance.

Rather than stepping away from her like she assumed he would, Cole gathered her closer, not allowing her to wriggle out before her father could reach them.

"Cole." Andrew slapped his hands together in front of him and rubbed them back and forth. A greedy, nasty smile stretched across his chubby face, turning Brianna's stomach even more. "You two look quite chummy. If I might ask, how are things going?"

He leaned closer to them and Brianna tried to step back out of his reach but Cole held fast, keeping one arm locked around the good side of her waist. She could smell her father's alcohol-laden breath as he spoke out of the corner of his mouth.

"Not giving you any trouble is she?"

Cole hugged her closer to him and Brianna closed her eyes in embarrassment. How could he be so...disgusting? She was his daughter for God's sake.

"*She* is standing right here, and you have yet to acknowledge her. A shame really, in front of all these people." Cole's chest rumbled against her back.

Andrew looked ready to explode. His jaw tensed and his eyes took on a menacing glow which clashed with his crimson cheeks. Without turning to her he murmured, "Brianna."

To the left, Brianna saw Tyler coming toward them with an intent look on his face, and limping still from yesterday's run-in with the curb. The thing had swollen to enormous proportions, but like a typical man, Ty would not let them take him in to have it x-rayed. Scottie was close behind, his hand on Ty's elbow as they made their way through the crowd. A commotion on the raised landing to her right had her twisting back the other way.

Caroline.

Brianna's heart pounded, betraying her desire not to show her anxiety.

Elegantly dressed in a long, white ball gown, her hair perfectly coifed, Caroline stood at the top of the two steps searching the crowd. Several men dressed discreetly in black tie were standing unobtrusively at attention, awaiting further instructions.

The vixen's gaze swept over them, leaving goose bumps parading up and down every inch of Brianna's skin. Caroline's head snapped back to them and her eyes flashed in anger as she took in the way Cole was wrapped so possessively around her. She descended the steps in regal fashion, attracting everyone's attention, including Andrew, who turned to stare.

"Cole." Brianna forced her throat to work. This woman would not intimidate her. She would not.

"Shh. In a few minutes, this will all be over."

Must be nice to be so confident.

With a finger, he tilted Brianna's face back to his and placed his lips on hers, easily parting her mouth with his tongue and insinuating it deep inside so it slid deliciously with her own. Her knees shook. No one would mistake this kiss.

Nor the fact that Cole lifted her left arm across her chest until her hand rested on her right shoulder, nicely displaying the two-carat rock and wedding band adorning her ring finger.

With Cole's tongue still dancing in her mouth, Brianna heard more than one gasp, several people applauding and many more, "Congratulations." She didn't care. His mouth was magical, his kisses exquisite. A fire-breathing dragon couldn't force her away from this all-consuming kiss. She lifted her hand

and raked her fingers through Cole's hair, holding him in place, and turned her body within his arms.

No dragons needed. It was the ear-piercing shriek that finally had them pulling apart, if for nothing else than to cover their ears.

"You whore!" Caroline leapt toward them, her hair and gown flapping behind her.

Brianna made a grave mistake by turning the wrong direction out of Cole's arms, and into the direct path of the screaming madwoman. Caroline raised her arm and swung before Cole could react. Her open palm landed squarely on Brianna's cheek with enough force the entire mansion could hear it.

Brianna stumbled backward, teetering on the silly heels Cole had asked her to wear. She reached out as Cole lunged for her but they missed each other and she ended up on the floor amidst the crowd of onlookers. Tears of pain welled in her eyes as she held one hand to her already bruised cheek throbbing with the tingling of a thousand needles and the other to the burning in her stitched-up side.

"You bitch. I told you what I'd do."

"Shut up, Caroline." Tyler wrestled his arms around Caroline's flailing limbs and twisted until they were locked behind her back. Brianna caught a glimmer of silver as Ty pulled something out of his back pocket.

The tears blurred her vision, but she heard the distinct click of handcuffs over Caroline's violent protests demanding Tyler to let her go. Then there were four more men, each eager to take over the squealing blonde. Brianna struggled to stand, with Cole's help, on her shaky legs.

"Christ, baby, are you okay?"

She nodded. Caroline had hit her, knocked her on her ass and was still fighting the group of men who each had a hand on her. Brianna stood there in total shock. Until this moment she had tried hard to believe Caroline couldn't really be responsible for the two earlier attacks, despite what Cole and Tyler both thought.

Now everything was clear to her. There could be no more denial, no more wishing it had been a simple robbery gone bad, or an out of control car. What a naïve little world she lived in. Another woman had actually tried, twice, to have her killed in a possessive fit over a man. She shivered at the memories.

"He's mine! I told you. He's mine," Caroline screamed.

* * *
** ** **

Cole was pissed. As if Bri hadn't gone through enough this week. He fought to keep his hands at his sides when what he wanted to do was put his fist through Caroline's nose. He'd never hit a woman in anger, hadn't been raised that way, and wasn't going to start now. Not even as sorely tempted as he was.

He stepped toward the still shrieking but contained blonde, when Andrew Wyatt pushed him out of the way.

"It's about time you stood up for your daughter," Cole growled. Maybe the man had some sense after all. It wouldn't have surprised Cole any if the man had done nothing, but then his reputation would be torn to shreds if he didn't defend his daughter with these people as witnesses.

Andrew not only didn't acknowledge Cole, he ignored him completely. Instead he stopped in front of Caroline, lifted his hand and slapped her across the face, paralyzing the woman and shocking not only Cole, but also the entire audience.

"Control yourself, Caroline. I will not allow any child of mine to make such a spectacle of themselves," he spat at her.

Not, "I will not allow anyone to make a spectacle of my child, but I will not allow any child of mine to make a spectacle of themselves."

"Holy shit." Cole's mouth fell open at the bomb Andrew had just dropped. Tyler looked just as floored. Cole heard a gasp and turned to see Bri, pale beneath her reddened cheek, her hand covering her mouth. Her big, watery eyes revealed her own surprised state.

"But you said he would be *mine*." Caroline stamped her foot, whining through the silent hush which fell over the crowd.

Cole and Tyler had expected Caroline was behind the attacks on Brianna all along, but never this. There had been nothing to suggest Caroline and Wyatt were related. At least it explained how Caroline supposedly had information about Lydia Wyatt.

"No, I said I wanted an heir." Andrew whirled on Brianna and shoved a thick forefinger at her. "You've messed this up, girl. This," he grabbed her hand and yanked at the ring on her finger, "was not supposed to happen. I asked him to sleep with you, not marry you."

A commotion rippled through the ballroom, ending the shocked silence.

"Get your hands off her," Cole growled. The fist he'd contained earlier was now a prominent fixture at the end of his arm. He might not hit a woman, but nothing would stop him from decking another man.

Andrew's face flushed as he realized what he'd said and how many people had heard him. His gaze darted around the room and he flung Bri's hand away as if she had burnt him.

"You're nothing better than a whore," he hissed. Apparently the man didn't know when to quit digging his hole.

Cole cocked his arm, ready to throw a punch, when a battle cry rang out to his right, diverting his attention.

"You bastard." Scott dove in the direction of his father, landing squarely on the bigger man's chest and knocking both of them to the ground with his momentum.

"Scottie." Bri charged at the two men writhing on the floor, but Cole pulled her back. "He's going to get hurt," she yelled, and tried to free herself from his grasp.

Somehow Scott managed to wind up on top and let loose a series of punches on the father he couldn't even see. Several missed, but many landed. Blood spurted from Andrew's nose and his lip split open before he was able to flip the two of them.

Tyler was on him before Andrew could get his arms untangled. He had Wyatt on the floor, belly down, his arms behind his back and locked in another pair of handcuffs in a matter of seconds. Then Ty stood, heavily favoring his bad ankle, and helped Scott to his feet.

"You okay, pal?"

Scott was breathing hard, but he smiled and nodded. "Yeah." He cracked his neck with two sharp turns of his head. "That felt good."

"Humph. Remind me not to get in a fist fight with you." Tyler laughed.

"This is not funny. God, don't you ever do that again, Scottie." Bri hugged him so hard Cole was sure the kid's head would pop off. Scott took the embrace with a grimace, squirming to get his arms unpinned.

"He called you a whore, squirt."

She looked at him. "So what? He has never said anything nice to me in twenty-six years, I didn't expect him to tonight. Especially with the marriage."

"Yeah, well, I couldn't let him get away with it one more time, Brianna. How's your head?" Scott lifted his head and turned like he was looking around the room. "I'd like to get my hands on Caroline too, if I could see the bitch."

Bri laughed then, releasing the heavy weight from Cole's chest. She would be all right.

"You will not hit a girl," she said.

"Our father did." He hung his head.

"And you are not him, thank God. I raised you better than that."

"Thank you, squirt. For everything." He bear hugged her shoulders and lifted her off her feet.

"Eeek. Put me down, put me down." Bri squealed when he spun her around.

The chief of police stepped forward and cleared his throat. "Do you want to press charges, ma'am?"

Scott set Bri on her feet, steadying her when she swayed beneath his touch. Cole took over, pulling her into his arms, her back to his chest, and settled his chin on top of her head. He couldn't stand not touching her.

"He attacked me," Andrew shouted, furiously angling his head in Scott's direction. Two men were dragging him off his knees. He shook with indignation, scattering droplets of the red river still running from his nose. Both men jerked back, unwilling to be tainted with his blood.

"I didn't see anything." The chief glanced around the room. "Did any of you see anything?" There was a chorus of no and a whole lot of head shaking.

"I saw everything. Don't worry, Father, I know what happened." Caroline stuck her pompous nose in the air.

"Shut up," he hissed at her.

"Ms. Grady, you have the right to remain silent, anything you say can and will be used against you..." The patrolman guided the sputtering Caroline away.

"I didn't do anything," she screeched. "He told me to. Daddy!" They could still hear her screaming out the door.

"Just do what you have to do about tonight's incident, Chief, I'll talk to Bri about the rest of it later. I want him out of our sight."

"Sure thing, Mr. Masters." He spoke to the patrolmen who had Andrew. "Take him in."

Chapter Eleven

Brianna swore to herself it wasn't the instant twinge of jealousy at hearing a woman's voice coming from the dining room that stopped her about halfway down the stairs. She wasn't the least bit curious as to why there would be a strange woman sharing their breakfast. No, it was definitely the soreness of her body from her and Cole's rough lovemaking session this morning making her halt on a dime.

Yeah, right.

She gripped the railing until her knuckles turned white. There was no reason to suspect their guest of being anything less than an old friend. Or maybe someone who worked for Ty. Yes that was it.

Of course the last time Brianna had come down the stairs to a woman's voice, she'd come face to face with the devil.

Then she heard it. A high-pitched laugh. Her breath caught and her eyes watered. It was a laugh she hadn't heard for more than sixteen years, and thought she would never hear again. It was a sound that filled her dreams and birthday wishes more times than she could count. The one thing she truly remembered from a childhood fraught with nannies and servants instead of parents.

Could it be? Had Caroline been telling her the truth that day at Tonio's?

She took a tentative step down, terrified she would trip and shatter the illusion of her mother's laugh. Or that she'd get there too fast and her hopes would be dashed when she saw someone who was not Lydia Wyatt at all.

Somehow she found herself standing before the dining room door, holding her breath. She didn't even remember descending the steps or crossing the foyer.

The door swung open and Brianna jumped.

"Hey, there you are, baby. I was just coming to get you."

Cole held out a hand to her and she stared at it. Maybe she was hearing things after all.

"Bri, you're looking a little pale." He leaned closer to her but she was paralyzed, unable to even lift her head for the kiss Cole offered her. "Hey, I wasn't too rough this morning, was I?" He smiled at her and grabbed her face with both hands. The kiss he placed on her mouth was gentle.

"Who's here, Cole?" she whispered when his lips touched hers.

He straightened and, with his thumb, wiped away a tear falling from her lashes. "Ty's been doing a lot of work this week—"

"Brianna?"

Brianna closed her eyes and swallowed. Her chin trembled. Cole stepped to the side. An angel in the form of Lydia Wyatt stood in front of her now, surrounded by the sunlight pouring through the opposite windows.

"Mama?"

"Isn't this great, squirt?" Scottie wrapped his arms around Brianna from behind and squeezed her, mindful of her stitches. "Ty found Mom for us."

More tears fell as she stared at their mother. How could he sound so happy? The woman, who was looking at them like she'd never left, had abandoned him as a tiny baby. Had walked out on her two children, leaving them with an evil man to fend for themselves. Had left her oldest child to take the place of her youngest child's mother.

Brianna nearly choked on all the years of hurt and pain she'd been through, when all along her mother was safe and alive. Why hadn't she fought for them? What kind of mother would do that to her kids?

"How..." She cleared her throat, dislodging the emotion clogging her windpipe. "Where..."

"Oh, sweetheart. Oh, God, I'm so sorry." Lydia moved forward, her arms outstretched, and enveloped Brianna and Scottie, who was still attached to her back.

Brianna stood like a stone between them and sought out Cole's face. She didn't find a smile there, but rather a look telling her he understood what she was feeling. Maybe he did, but she didn't. Then he moved and placed a hand on her mother's back.

"Let's sit down," he said.

Lydia let go of her children, sniffed, and wiped the tears off her cheeks, then nodded at Cole.

"I think that would be a good idea." She wobbled a bit and Cole shot a hand out to steady her.

Brianna was glad he was in control because she was still shell-shocked. Scottie marched her forward, his arms still surrounding her until they reached a seat where Cole took over and gently forced her to sit. He pulled out another chair and placed it between hers and Lydia's, forming a triangle for the three of them.

Cole maneuvered Scottie to his chair before stepping into the middle and reaching for her hands again. Brianna let him take them and pull her up to stand. With a small nudge, Brianna found herself in front of her mother. So close their knees touched. He placed his hands on her waist and guided her backward until her knees buckled and she was sitting in his lap. She never took her eyes off the elegantly dressed woman facing her.

Lydia patted her thighs and swallowed. Brianna cocked her head at the telltale gesture. The same one she and Scottie both had. It made her seem somehow more real. She was just as nervous and anxious about this meeting as Brianna was.

"Sweetheart." Lydia swallowed again, so loud Brianna heard it. "I spoke with Scottie this morning. He and I both had a good cry." Her smile was sad. There were things you could never make up for, Brianna guessed.

"Andrew had her locked away in an institution, squirt." Scottie's voice was soft beside her.

A small chunk of ice which had been forming around her heart broke off. If her blind brother who'd never known his mother could reconcile with her, then Brianna could put forth every effort to do so herself.

"Why? Why would he do that?" Her throat was dry and tight. That's why the croakiness.

Cole brushed the hair from her neck. "Just listen, baby. She's going to explain it all. I wanted you and Scott to be together, but he ran into her when Ty brought her in and you were...well you were otherwise occupied at the time."

Brianna's face flushed. She knew exactly how occupied she'd been. She glanced at her mother and was shocked to see her trying to hide a smile.

Another chunk melted.

"Oh, honey. Andrew was demented, truly mad. I guess I just didn't see it until it was too late. He was obsessed with having a boy." Lydia reached over and threaded her fingers with Scottie's. Brianna watched him return her grip and a knot formed in her throat. Her brother was taking to their mother like she'd never been gone. She was happy for him. Happy he could come to peace with her so quickly.

"We tried so hard after you to have Scott, but there were complications." Her face twisted with a mixture of pain and anger. "He wasn't good enough for your father," she choked out. "His fixation grew and grew until finally he was forcing me to..." She dislodged her hand from Scottie's and blew her nose on a napkin.

"I was suffering from postpartum depression. Something your father denied with every breath. And maybe it had nothing to do with postpartum, maybe I was just depressed all around. I don't know." She sniffed again.

"Scott was only six months old, dear God. My baby. He was so small and had so many problems and that bastard wouldn't let me see him, or you. Night after night, day after day, I suffered his touch. I begged and pleaded, but he was bent and deranged. He kept telling me over and over how much better Scott was in the hands of his nurses."

Her body shook and she cried out, burying her face in her hands.

"I swear to you, I didn't know there were no nurses. I swear."

"Mama," Brianna breathed, feeling her renewed pain, disgusted by what she was hearing. She slid off Cole's lap and knelt in front of her mother. "I'm sorry, Mama. I'm sorry you had to go through all that." She grasped her mother's hands and tugged them off her face.

"No, sweetheart, it's me that's sorry. I should have done more, protected you two somehow. I didn't know what his plans were, that he was working on having me committed. And the women. There were so many, in and out of our home. I did my best to shield you from all of them."

"It's okay, Mama." The huge weight lifted from Brianna's shoulders as she patted her mother on the back. All of the guilt and anger was gone. Her mother had tried, had done the best she could under the circumstances. "Me and Scottie, we turned out okay," she consoled. "Scottie's a good man, Mama, and any other man would be proud to call him their son."

Lydia burst out again, "Thanks to you, Brianna. You've done a wonderful job raising him. You're going to be a great mother someday."

Her chin and bottom lip shook and she looked deep into Brianna's eyes. So deep she could swear the woman saw to the bottom of her soul.

"It's despicable what he forced you into doing with Mr. Mas...your husband." A grin split her face. "My baby's married," she squealed. "I'm sorry I missed it, darling."

Cole cleared his throat behind Brianna. "I don't think it turned out too despicable."

She turned around and slapped his leg.

Scottie snorted. "You wouldn't."

She smacked his leg too. "Stop it both of you." She and Lydia laughed.

"Hmm. I wonder what Ty would say," Scottie continued.

"He would say ditto," Tyler announced, peeling away from the wall. Her heart gave a jolt. She hadn't even known he was in the room. He was supported by two crutches, a by-product of the emergency room visit she'd demanded last night when all the guests had left and he could put no weight on his ankle at all. It was amazing how quickly he'd capitulated about the doctor when she'd withheld easing any future hard-ons until he went. The injury had turned out to be a very bad sprain and now he was under orders to stay off it completely for the next week at least.

After the ER visit, he'd gotten in a car with a driver and disappeared. She missed having him in their bed last night. Because of her mother, she knew why he hadn't been there.

She jumped off her knees and darted between her mother and Scottie to give him a hug.

"Thank you, Ty, for finding my mother and bringing her here."

"Anytime, little one."

They looked at each other, each wanting to kiss, but not sure if they should in front of Lydia. Ty finally bent down and pecked at her cheek, leaving her feeling awkward. She wished they didn't have to hide.

"Later, little one," he whispered.

"Please, don't mind me," Lydia said.

Brianna whipped her head around, still caught up in Ty's arms. She hadn't really heard her mother say that had she?

Lydia gave a dainty cough, her face pink, as she searched the face of each occupant in the room, then shrugged. "Umm, Scott mentioned some things to me earlier when we talked." Her cheeks grew rosier. "And, while I was a tad concerned at first, Scott went on to tell me exactly the way things were and how happy you are here with...both your men. He then threatened me with death if I were to do anything to compromise said happiness."

Cole and Tyler both cracked up, each having been threatened the same way. Brianna stood with her hands on her hips and contemplated just what to do with her sneaky little brother and his interfering ways. Nothing. She could do nothing to the boy who sat grinning over his shoulder at her like a Cheshire cat.

Lydia stood and walked toward Brianna. Tyler twisted her around so her back was against his front and put his hands on her shoulders. Every few seconds a snort would erupt from his nose. If the man didn't stop laughing she was going to smack him too!

"Sweetheart. I am the last person on Earth to give advice about relationships, and to tell the truth, I've been away from society for so long, I don't even know what is apropos anymore. I suspect, with the lack of a wedding ring on Mr. Cannon's finger, this isn't something you want to share with the world. But I will be the last person to stop you from having a relationship with two men, if that's what you want. If that's what the three of you want."

Brianna cried. Having her mother's acceptance meant the world to her. Tyler squeezed her shoulders.

"Now then, that being said, gentlemen, if either of you hurts my daughter…"

"Yes, ma'am." Cole nodded his acknowledgement of her warning.

"Ditto," Tyler said.

"I'll be right next to you, Mom," Scottie piped in, standing up.

There was a chorus of "shut up" from the three of them. Lydia looked amused.

"All right then. Seeing as last night was a long one for me, I am going to have a rest. I'll see you all later for lunch."

Brianna threw her arms around her mother as she passed. "I love you, Mama. Welcome home."

"Thank you, sweetheart. Your husband…s, have offered me a suite here at the house until I get my feet back."

"I wouldn't expect anything different from them. Please, stay as long as you like."

"I will."

Epilogue

Cole stood and arched his arms above his head, popping the length of his spine. The last two weeks had been long and full of a mixture of tears and laughter. Mother and children were in the process of bonding after long years of separation, but all three seemed to be adjusting well despite Bri's shaky start.

He looked at her now curled up in the armchair, her nose stuck in some sappy romance novel. The strap of her camisole—he guessed that's what you'd call the thin cotton top she was wearing—had slipped off, leaving the creamy skin of her shoulder bare.

"Time for bed, Bri." He couldn't contain a low growl that had her head snapping up. Her gaze traveled the length of his body, widening when they reached his groin and the tent of his sweatpants. Her nostrils flared and the tip of her little, pink tongue darted out to lick her bottom lip.

Without a word she dog-eared the page she was on, tossed the paperback onto the end table, and peeled out of the chair. He held his hand out, silently beckoning her to him, and felt a stab of déjà vu. They'd done this before in this exact room, the first day, three weeks before, when he'd asked her to trust him with her body and her mind.

Five days after meeting her, she'd become his wife.

She smiled seductively at him, making his cock twitc̶ nipples were drawn tight and puckered against the fabric ̶ pajama shirt.

His voice was hoarse when he spoke, affirming his need f̶ her. "If there weren't other people in this house right now, I'd have you laid out on this floor and be buried in you already."

She took his hand. "Where's Ty?"

"Shower."

He led her up the stairs and into their bedroom, and turned to lock the door. Seconds later, he had her right where he wanted her. Spread out like a feast across their bed. Just yesterday she'd gotten the stitches removed from her side. He fisted his hands at the angry red welt marring her soft skin.

Both Caroline and her father would be serving some sort of time, probably only community service for Andrew, for everything that had happened. Caroline, on the other hand would most likely see the inside of a jail cell. She had hired the men who had tried two times to kill Brianna, and had stupidly pleaded to her lawyer how she would do it again.

Andrew still maintained he didn't know anything about Caroline's misdeeds, but he did admit he'd fueled the woman into action by giving her the information about Bri's mother.

He'd wanted a son and had schemed to ensure at least one by pitting Caroline and Bri against one another, knowing Caroline already had a vested interest in Cole. Caroline's reward for conceiving first was to be publicly acknowledged by Andrew as his daughter. It had been enough to think she might someday be a beneficiary of the Wyatt estate, so she'd gone along with the man's plans.

Right now the two were embroiled in a he said, she said debate on who actually knew what. Caroline said her father told her to get rid of Brianna by any means necessary, Andrew ʌ he told her no such thing, only that she better hurry if ,anted to get her hands on Cole.

It didn't look like anyone would ever know the truth.

"You're wearing too many clothes."

Bri's huskily spoken words snapped his mind back to the task at hand. Fucking his wife. Since the party he hadn't been able to keep his hands off her. They'd come too close to losing her, twice. He still wasn't comfortable letting her leave his sight.

He smiled at her. "I'll see if I can't accommodate you." He quickly shed his sweatpants and T-shirt, and crawled onto the bed between her spread thighs. Her naked pussy was shiny with the moisture already pooling there. They both heard the shower turn off and glanced at the bathroom door.

He returned his attention to her drenched cunt. "Ty'll be here any minute."

"I can't wait." She licked her lips and he groaned.

"Neither can I." He spread the pouty outer lips of her slick vagina with his thumbs and speared her with his tongue, lapping at the sweet honey.

"Oh, God." Her hands seized at his hair, pulling his head closer to her heat.

He continued licking her core, dragging and swirling his tongue over and around and in her, but never quite touching the one place where he knew she would want him the most.

"Cole, please." Her chest bellowed with every pant.

"I was hungry for a little late-night sandwich." Tyler, still a little shaky on his bad ankle, hobbled over and joined them on the bed, nude, one hundred percent aroused, and still damp from his shower.

Cole murmured against her clit. "Sandwich sounds good to me too." He blew on the heated flesh and held Bri down with an arm across her hips when she bowed off the bed.

Tyler latched onto one of her nipples and sucked the bead into his mouth. Her other breast received attention from his fingers.

Cole eyed his wife and best friend from his position between her thighs, all the while plundering her juicy pussy with his tongue and fingers.

"No." Bri's head whipped from side to side on her pillow. "No sandwich until you let me come."

He and Tyler lifted their heads simultaneously. He arched an eyebrow at her.

"Excuse me?"

"Did she really just say that?" Ty asked him.

Bri jackknifed to a sitting position and latched on to the nearest man to her, Tyler. She grabbed both of his ears and leaned in 'til her nose touched his.

"You heard what I said."

"I think she's serious, Cole."

"Naw, what made you think that?"

"Me first," she ground out. She was gritting her teeth so hard Cole was surprised they didn't break. Then she casually let go of Ty's ears like she hadn't just threatened him with dismemberment and lay back down. "Please."

Tyler shook his head.

Within a heartbeat Cole reversed their positions, making Bri squeal as he flipped her around. Now he was on his back, Bri was straddling his hips and Ty was behind her. Both their cocks were poised at her entrances.

"That was so not fair," she grumbled and commenced pounding on his pecs with her tight, little fists.

Tyler laughed. Cole easily corralled her punches and pulled on her wrists until her elbows were up by his ears and she was draped flat across him. The action had somehow moved her just enough so the engorged head of his cock slipped inside her sheath. She capitulated as he sank into her further and sighed against his throat.

"That feels so good."

Cole chuckled. "You're a greedy little wench tonight." He laughed again when she shrugged. He trailed his fingertips down her arms and over her shoulders while Tyler readied himself and her for his rear penetration.

Brianna wiggled on top of him, crawling down his body to impale herself on his erection. He didn't even try to bite back the moan clawing its way from his groin.

Tyler swatted her butt, making her jump and squeak.

"Be still, little one."

From his mound of pillows, propped-up position, Cole watched over her shoulder as Tyler separated the cheeks of her ass and placed the tube of lubricant at her opening. She squirmed again when he gave the tube a squeeze.

"Just the lube, Bri," Tyler crooned. "Be still for me and let me get inside you." With a dollop of lube on his palm, he took his cock in hand, spreading the oil until it glistened and a pearly drop of come appeared on the broad, purpled head.

Tyler bent forward, spreading her bottom again, and pressed into the rosy opening. Sweat beaded his best friend's forehead and chest as he sank into her.

Her hands fisted in the sheets on either side of his head. "Oh God, oh God," she chanted.

Cole continued stroking her back. "Relax baby, let us make you feel good."

Tyler's cock slid against his own with only the thin barrier of tissue between them.

"It's too much," she screamed even though she was pushing back, engaging them further inside her.

"It's not enough, little one," Tyler hissed.

Cole reciprocated. "It'll never be enough."

"Fuck. I gotta move, Cole."

"Yes!" Bri lifted her head. Her eyes were wild. "Move. Somebody, move. Now!"

They set up a rhythm of thrusting and Cole reached up to fondle her nipples, tweaking and pinching while she grunted between them.

"So good. So good. Don't...stop."

"Can't," Tyler panted.

His balls slapped against Cole's with each lunge, tightening them to the point of pain. Tyler's hand skated across his abdomen on its way to Bri's clit. She screamed when he found it, the touch setting off an explosive climax that ripped through her convulsing body.

Her pussy pulsed wildly on his dick, milking him and dragging his orgasm to fruition. Apparently it did the same for Tyler because he shouted above them, the tendons in his neck cording as he threw his head back.

Both of them slammed into her one last time and held themselves rigid as hot jets of their come flooded her sweet body.

She collapsed on him, exhausted. Tyler fell forward, catching himself on his hands, and rocked slowly against her, squeezing out every bit of his orgasm.

"I love you, Brianna Masters." Cole kissed her sweaty temple and wiped the damp strands of hair from her face.

"And I love you."

Cole felt Tyler disengage himself from Bri's sated body before he bent over and placed his lips on her shoulder.

"And *I* love you, Brianna Masters."

Brianna's cheeks tickled Cole's throat when she smiled.

"Ditto, Tyler Cannon."

Tyler laughed at her use of his favorite word and rolled to his side.

Cole pulled out of the warmth of her pussy reluctantly. He shifted them so her back was snug against Ty's chest and she faced him. He rested his hand on her hip and Tyler wound his arm along her belly. They all breathed hard.

"Just think, all this because your father wanted an heir."

Tyler snorted.

"Mmmhmm." Her palm flattened on his chest. "I think he may have gotten his wish."

Cole's heart stopped. He lifted her face to his with a finger under her chin and caught Ty's shocked stare over her shoulder.

"What are you saying, baby?"

She shrugged as if they were having a casual conversation. He wanted to shake her for being so obtuse.

"I'm usually very regular."

"And," Ty rasped.

"I was supposed to start a few days ago."

Cole swept his hand up next to Tyler's and they covered the place where their child might be growing. Then he paled. Damn. They'd had some really rough sex in the last couple of days.

"Of course, it could be all the stress I've been under, but the timing would not have been off those first few times we were together." She smiled shyly at him and then at Tyler, who still looked awestruck. "So?"

"A baby." Cole grinned, a big, stupid grin. "Bring her on."

"Her?" Tyler and Bri echoed.

All three of them burst out laughing.

Annmarie McKenna

Annmarie McKenna lives just outside St. Louis, MO with her husband and four kids. Between shuttling her kids from school to sports, and various other activities, she is planted in front of her computer reading, or writing her next story.

She would love to hear from you. To learn more about Annmarie McKenna, please visit www.annmariemckenna.com, or send an email to annmarmck@yahoo.com.

Look for these new titles from
Annmarie McKenna

Seeing Eye Mate ~ Fall, 2006
Checkmate ~ Winter, 2007
Two Sighted ~ Spring, 2007

Shy girls need to talk dirty too...
Enjoy this excerpt from

Talk Dirty To Me

(c) 2006 Michelle Miles

*A contemporary romance novella available from Samhain
Publishing.*

"Hi, my name is Trixie."

"Trixie." The deep, baritone voice on the other end sounded
as though he tested her name on his tongue. "I like that name."

"Do you? What's your name?" She put on her sexiest phone
voice, the one that could curl men's toes. Claudia Anderson
easily slipped into her Trixie guise as she picked up her nail
polish. Squeezing the phone between her neck and shoulder,
she continued polishing her toes.

"Jack," he replied. He already sounded breathless.

"Is this your first time, Jack?"

"Uh...yeah." His voice dropped to a whisper.

"Are you married, love?" She lowered her voice to match
his.

"Ooh...I like that. Call me that again."

"Sure, love. Are you married?"

"No."

"Oh, good. A single man. I like single men." She finished
painting her big toe and moved on, making sure she got a good
coat on her second. "Tell me what you like, love."

"Redheads," he said.

"Really? Well, I'm a redhead." Not really, but she always
gave a man what he wanted.

"A natural redhead?" His voice shook, as if the thought of
her being a redhead really turned him on.

"Of course."

"Can I see sometime?"

"You naughty boy." She laughed her fake laugh and rolled her eyes. It was against her rules to fraternize with the clients, except via telephone. "Tell me, Jack, what else you like."

"I'd like to fuck you from behind."

"Really?" She paused, staring at herself in the mirror. Her brown, almond-shaped eyes stared back, mascara smudged underneath them. Usually men warmed up to the idea of talking dirty. This one, he got straight to the point. She liked that. She smiled. "Does that turn you on?"

"Oh, yeah."

"What else?"

"Are you naked?"

"*Of course.*" What the hell...he didn't know. Another glance in the bureau mirror confirmed she wore her favorite long, navy-blue t-shirt. She continued to paint her toes, moving from the right foot to the left. She had done this for so long, she no longer got excited.

"I'd like to lick you."

An unexpected heat washed over her. Without him being specific, even. She clutched the phone, gripping it hard in her hand as her other hovered over a half-painted toenail.

"I bet you taste sweet, too," he breathed.

Her nipples hardened, straining against the well-worn fabric of her shirt. "That's what I've been told. Do you like oral sex, Jack?"

"I like to give and receive, baby."

Ooohhh. His response made the blood drain from her head. Her vision wavered and she swayed, thankful she was sitting down. What was it about this man on the other end of the phone that excited her? His voice? His words? She didn't know. She didn't really care either.

"I've got my dick in my hand," he purred. "Tell me what to do."

"Stroke yourself, love," she whispered, her voice edged with passion. "Rub your thumb over the damp tip." She could just picture it. His thick length in her hand...

"Oh, yeah."

"Now...what do you want me to do?"

"What do you feel like? I want to know."

His voice purred the words and she paused. There it was again. That tingling sensation sneaking up and down her. No other caller had caused such an uproar.

"Soft and silky." Claudia stuck the nail brush back into the bottle and screwed on the lid, setting it on her nightstand.

"Are you wet?"

Wet and ready for sex. She knew exactly how wet but she didn't want to acknowledge it. There was an incessant throbbing between her legs, begging for her to touch, to feel.

"Touch yourself." His voice urged her on, making her want to.

Arousal prickled her skin. Heart pounding, she slipped her hand beneath her satin panties. Her index finger slid between her slick folds, feeling a moistness that surprised her. She stifled a gasp as her heart rammed against her breastbone.

"*Very* wet, love." Wetter than she had been in a long while.

"Mmmm."

He paused and she waited, letting her finger glide over her dampness. It had been so long since she'd had a man, she had forgotten what it was like.

"I'd like your mouth on my dick right now."

"Okay. Your dick is in my mouth and I'm licking you up and down. Using the tip of my tongue."

She heard a little rumble of a groan on the other end of the phone. Maybe she had spent too much time with her vibrator.

Maybe it was time to get out there and see what was on the market these days.

"And what else?" Jack asked.

"I take you into my mouth, all the way to the back of my throat, and suck you. Hard."

"Ooooo."

"You're nice and big, aren't you?"

"Nine inches," he boasted. Men always loved to boast about their penis size.

Claudia was suddenly aware of a familiar tightness in her lower abdomen and knew she was close to orgasm. She squeezed the phone between her shoulder and ear, then slipped out of her panties and tossed them on the shag carpet. Leaning back into the pillows, she slid her hand over her throbbing mound.

"Are you still touching yourself?" he asked, breaking into her thoughts.

Was she ever. She wanted him to keep talking. Closing her eyes, she could picture his face. Strong features. Lean form. Nice kissable lips and a good kisser. So...*manly.*

"Yes." She was like a first timer panting into the phone. She tried to control her reaction, but her heart pounded harder in her chest. "Tell me more."

"I'd like to slide my tongue over your clit, lick you up in down in slow, long strokes while I finger you. How about that?"

"Umm." He struck her speechless, something unusual for a phone sex operator.

"You like that, don't you?" His voice wavered, sending sparks through her.

What the hell is going on? She actually liked this man on the other end of the phone. The sound of his voice sent a warm shiver through her, making her body stand up and take notice.

"Then I'll stick my dick in you and slow fuck you."

"*Oh.*" She breathed the word. On the other end, his own breathing increased. She opened her knees and lifted her hips into her hand.

"Oh!" she gasped.

"You're coming, baby, aren't you?"

"Yes!"

"Wait for me. Here I come. I'm coming."

She glanced down at the rumpled T-shirt up around her breasts and her hand moving back and forth over her own sex. She gasped, then emitted a loud moan as her body contracted, her legs closing as the spasms overtook her. Her toes curled and she shuddered against her fingers at Jack's own groan of pleasure on the other end.

"Wow, baby, that was great."

She panted, trying to catch her breath. She curled her knees to her chest and rolled to her side, still holding the phone. "Thank you, Jack, for calling."

The standard line she used when faking an orgasm took on a whole new meaning.

Remembering her damp toenails, she glanced down. *Shit!* Now she'd have to start over again.

But it was worth it.

He's a shape-shifting wolf, she's a psychic and his other half. In order to catch a killer, Caelen has to rely on his Seeing Eye Mate. Coming to Samhain Publishing October 24, 2006.

Enjoy this excerpt from

Seeing Eye Mate

Caelan drew a breath and steadied himself after the sucker punch to his gut. The woman could pack a wallop with her diminutive frame. He re-holstered his gun and spared a chuckle for the caveman routine he'd just engaged in. It had to have something to do with his species, and their innate sense to protect their mate.

Of course, he should have picked up on the fact that she'd been so nonchalant when saying she'd been attacked. Instead he'd gone into lockdown mode and prepared to defend her life with his own.

He eyed the door with caution and wondered how she could accuse it of attacking her.

Following her retreating figure into the house, Caelan surveyed the area. It was, in a word, homey. His mouth quirked at the mess she hadn't wanted him to see, and he planted his hands on his hips. Tieran had disappeared. For a split second he thought about the fact that she might run, but dismissed the idea just as fast. Why would she have any reason to run?

He flipped the door closed behind him with his heel, and was surprised when it swung back and slapped him in the rear. Now he could see why she said the door had ambushed her. He pushed firmly on the paneled wood but it still wouldn't close. He frowned at it. It *was* possessed.

Caelan turned when an odd breeze wafted across the back of his neck. The hair on the rest of his body stood on end, a testimony to the eerie feeling he was being watched. His gaze traced the room carefully, looking for anything that may have caused the sudden puff of air, and he was tempted to start humming the theme from *The X-Files*.

"You have to turn the knob to close the door," Tieran yelled from somewhere deeper in the house.

How had she known he was having trouble with the door? *Because she lives here, you idiot.*

"Where are you?"

"In the kitchen." Her reply was muffled.

"The kitchen. I guess I'm on my own to find that." *Which shouldn't be too hard for an expert security person like yourself.*

He froze in the doorway to the kitchen at the sight greeting him. Tieran was bent over, her upper half hidden as she scrounged in the refrigerator. More blood rushed straight to his cock as he stared at her firm butt encased in tight blue jeans. The waistband of her jeans was bowed out, giving him a glimpse of skin at the small of her back.

His fingers itched to touch her and his inner wolf howled, wanting to claim its mate. Cael curled his hands into fists to keep from reaching out and taking what he already knew to be his.

He swallowed, remembering how her eyes had glittered and her cheeks grew rosy when she was angry. He'd first seen it last night, then again when he'd stood on her porch an inch away from her face. Would they look they same way when he was buried deep in her wet heat? Would they glaze over when a climax overtook her? He shifted in an attempt to ease himself.

"Since you're being so persistent, I guess I'll offer you a drink."

He had *not* made a sound, in fact, was well known for his sneaking ability. She either had supersonic hearing or a strong sixth sense.

Caelan rubbed a hand at the goose bumps suddenly tingling along his neck. "What do you have?" His voice cracked like a preteen in puberty, heating his face.

"Hmm. Water."

"Wow, great choices. What are you having?" he asked, regaining control before she could see the precarious hold he had on his libido.

"Mountain Dew." She rose and faced him, a green can in one hand.

His attention, however, was drawn to her midriff where her jeans, he just realized, were unbuttoned and unzipped. A slice of skin peeked out where her T-shirt had ridden up. It looked smooth as silk, just like her delectable backside had.

"What are you drooling over? You can't have my Mountain Dew."

His attention was still riveted on her belly and he found himself swallowing again. A tiny gem sparkled at him from where it nestled in her navel. It was the most perfect fucking thing he'd ever seen. He stalked toward her. She seemed to be completely oblivious to the effect she was having on him.

"Water's fine," he choked out. He gestured to the exposed part of her anatomy. "Your...umm...XYZ!" he spit out.

Her gaze dropped. "Oh, geez. I find it hard to believe you've never seen a female body before."

He looked to the table and back to her, unable to control his need for her. He could take her right there on the table.

Tieran threw her hands up. "Whoa!" Forgetting she was holding the can, she fumbled to fix her jeans.

The can fell to the floor at just the right angle and exploded, spraying the sticky, yellow soda everywhere.

"Ugh!" she yelled. Caelan was rooted to the floor, a silly grin on his face. "You!" she pointed. "Out. Go. Sit on the couch and wait for me."

"Uh-uh." He shook his head and continued walking towards her. She was soaked from head to toe, and he was going to enjoy licking every inch of her clean.

Her eyes widened and she stepped back, once, twice, and bumped into the counter behind her. He had her between his rock and a hard place.

"What are you doing?" she whispered.

"I'm going to kiss you." He stopped just in front of her, pinning her to the cabinets, and traced a line of soda down her cheek with his forefinger. "And you're going to kiss me back." He framed her face with both his hands, holding her in place, though he didn't need to. She was frozen to her spot.

Her lips were warm and soft as he licked along them, sipping a drop of the soda's sweetness from one corner. He pressed his tongue between her lips, demanding that she open to him, which she did without the slightest bit of hesitation.

He tasted her, dueled with her tongue, bit her bottom lip gently, until she groaned and her body melted into his.

Printed in the United States
148617LV00001B/90/A